"If we're going to start some new family traditions," Andrew said, "let's add one more. Let's have a dozen kids."

"A dozen?" Carrie gasped. "Isn't that going a bit far?"

He leered at her. "Think of all the fun we'll have. Someday we can tell little Andrew that he was conceived in the study, and little Carrie that she was conceived on the porch swing, and little Bryan or Edward or Sidney that he was conceived in the backyard under a maple tree—"

"Whoa!" Carrie held up a hand. "Aren't any going to be conceived in a bed?"

"One or two," he said, winking.

Carrie felt a tide of warmth flow over her...

Katherine Granger *was born in Massachusetts, has lived in Texas, and now resides in Connecticut. She has worked as an insurance training specialist, a hospital executive secretary, and a computer programmer. Aside from writing, her interests include reading, horseback riding, scouting out antiques and American folk art, and visiting New England country inns.*

Dear Reader:

One year ago, at a time when romance readers were asking for "something different," we took a bold step in romance publishing by launching an innovative new series of books about married love: TO HAVE AND TO HOLD.

Since then, TO HAVE AND TO HOLD has developed a faithful following of enthusiastic readers. We're still delighted to receive your letters—which come from teenagers, grandmothers, and women of every age in between, both married and single. All of you have one quality in common—you believe that love and romance exist beyond the "happily ever after" endings of more conventional stories.

In the months to come, we will continue to offer romance reading of the highest caliber in TO HAVE AND TO HOLD. Keep an eye out for two books by our very popular Jeanne Grant—*Cupid's Confederates* this month and *Conquer the Memories* next month. Jennifer Rose also returns in December with *Pennies From Heaven,* and Kate Nevins, whom some of you know as the author of several SECOND CHANCE AT LOVE romances, has written her first TO HAVE AND TO HOLD, *Memory and Desire,* coming in January. Be sure, too, not to overlook the "newcomers" you'll continue to see in TO HAVE AND TO HOLD. In December, Joan Darling debuts with *Tyler's Folly,* a unique, witty story that made me laugh out loud. We're proud to bring these wonderfully talented writers to you.

Warmest wishes,

Ellen Edwards

Ellen Edwards, Senior Editor
TO HAVE AND TO HOLD
The Berkley Publishing Group
200 Madison Avenue
New York, N.Y. 10016

PRIVATE LESSONS
KATHERINE GRANGER

SECOND CHANCE AT LOVE
BOOK

Other books by *Katherine Granger*

Second Chance at Love
A MAN'S PERSUASION   #89
. WANTON WAYS   #206

To Have and to Hold
MOMENTS TO SHARE   #13

To Have and to Hold books are published by
The Berkley Publishing Group
200 Madison Avenue, New York, NY 10016

To my brother, Bobby, and his new wife, Sharyn
—Mr. and Mrs. Robert E. Fanning—
May they long live in love and understanding

This is to acknowledge with special thanks the help of Susan B. Neuman, Assistant Professor of English at Eastern Connecticut State College, who helped me understand the complicated procedures of awarding tenure at universities. Any mistakes or misconceptions in this book are entirely due to my own ignorance.

1

CARRIE EVEREST SAT at one end of the elegant dining table, her elbows bracketing a delicate Wedgwood plate, her green eyes troubled as she watched her husband. Or rather as she watched the opened newspaper that shielded him from her view. Sixteen feet away he sat, lost in the morning news, pausing now and then to reach for his coffee, sip it, set the cup down again, and rattle the pages as he folded the paper to read the stock market report.

The honeymoon was definitely over, she thought wryly. For four weeks now, ever since returning from their month-long honeymoon tour of Greece and the Grecian islands, they had settled into this dreadful morning routine—each seated at one end of the sixteen-foot-long monster, which was how she thought of the gleaming Sheraton table. They were so far away from each other she practically needed a telephone to get Andrew's attention.

She sighed and let her gaze wander over the enormous room. It was undeniably beautiful, a formal room filled with the finest English and American antiques. Imported, hand-painted blue, white, and rust paper covered the walls above pristine white wainscoting, and a gleaming brass Williamsburg chandelier hung over the table. A fire crackled in the fireplace, chasing away the last vestiges of morning chill that the central heating had not yet banished. The table, its gleaming mahogany surface seeming to stretch into eternity, was set with snowy white linen placemats with dainty, hand-embroidered blue figures on the hand-sewn edges—the perfect foil for the elegant Wedgwood with its delicate border of blue, rust, and gold. A centerpiece of spring flowers arranged in a Waterford crystal bowl belied the frosty weather outdoors.

Carrie turned her head and looked out the French doors, past the brick terrace—now barren of its white wrought-iron patio furniture—out across the rolling snow-covered half acre of lawn to the ice-laden maples and oaks, which captured the morning sun and transformed the landscape to a fairyland of glistening beauty.

But here in the dining room all was orderly. The cavernous room fairly echoed its rich history. Carrie could just picture the Everest ancestors clustered around this same table, refined, cultured, their cold Yankee eyes unable to appreciate the natural beauty that lay just outside their windows and doors.

Sighing again, she noted the blue and white figured draperies that were drawn back to admit the early-morning sun. Savoring the meager warmth, she closed her eyes and breathed in deeply. When she opened her eyes she gazed at the brilliant path of sunlight stretching across the plush Oriental rug, ivory bordered with rust and blue Chinese figures—figures that stood for luck, Andrew had told her the morning after their honeymoon. She stared at the strange Chinese symbols, and a smile spread across her lips.

Luck. She would need all of it she could get. She had to break this morning ritual, had to stop the Everest ancestors from grabbing her and dragging her into this somber silence. She may have married an Everest, but she hadn't been born one. This was *her* home now, and by God, she intended to run it that way.

Then her shoulders slumped, and she glanced around the room, feeling the power of past Everests clutch at her. They were gone now, all except her beloved husband, Andrew; yet, they seemed to live on, filling the house with their spectral presences, forcing her usually ebullient spirit into a mold she hadn't been made for.

Carrie straightened her posture, raised her chin, and took a deep breath. She would start today. Right now. This morning. Before another day passed, before another morning could be ruined by the vast space that separated her from her wonderful husband. She trembled as she glanced down at the megaphone that rested out of sight just under the table. Yesterday it had seemed a wonderful idea. She had giggled on and off all day, picturing the shock that would claim Andrew's handsome face before hearty laughter overtook it. But now, sitting in the midst of the Everest domain, she wondered yet again if she were truly suited to being Andrew's wife.

The fear had developed slowly over the past month, silently, insidiously inserting itself into her thoughts. But she hadn't even been able to talk to her husband about it. And yet, instinctively she knew she must talk about it. Her marriage depended on it.

Deep breath. Shoulders back. Courage! Feeling her confidence return, she bent and picked up the megaphone—a conventional, cone-shaped mechanism of the type wielded by bouncing cheerleaders at Asquith University football games as they pranced and yelled for their team, seemingly oblivious to the autumn cold in the windy Connecticut stadium.

This morning, however, it would be put to a different use. Carrie suppressed a laugh. A *very* different use. Today it would herald a new beginning—the breaking of a hundred-year-old tradition in the Everest household.

She grinned devilishly as she raised the megaphone to her lips and shouted, "Ahoy down there!"

Sixteen feet away, Andrew Everest jumped up from his chair, *The Wall Street Journal* flying out of his hands to waft through the air and settle onto the Oriental carpet. He stood, dumbfounded, and stared down the length of the table, his reading glasses resting at a dangerous angle on his aristocratic nose.

"Carrie!" he exclaimed. "What on earth are you doing?" He reached up and removed his glasses, folded them carefully, and placed them on the table.

"Getting your attention," she said sweetly, leaning down to replace the megaphone on the floor.

Andrew began to gather up the newspaper, which was strewn all over the floor. Then he settled back into his chair, irritation fighting with a grin. The grin won. He shook his head admiringly. "My God, woman, what will you come up with next?"

"I'll stand on this damned table and strip if I must," she said staunchly, suppressing the nervous jitters in her stomach. It was now or never, sink or swim. She gestured expansively down the length of the gleaming table.

"Do you know what I'd have to do to reach across

this table and kiss you, Andrew Everest?" She made a pretense of stretching out her neck. "Become a giraffe, that's what!"

She shook her head rebelliously, fired up, knowing that she had begun and that nothing could stop her now. "Andrew, I feel as if we're in two different rooms! No, counties! You're way down there in Fairfield County, where spring comes three weeks earlier than up here in Hartford County, where I sit. We need telephones to converse—or, at the very least, carrier pigeons."

Andy sat back and rested his elbows on the arms of the Chippendale chair, his lips turned up in an amused smile. "Not pigeons, darling. Think what they'd do to the carpet."

"Damn the carpet!" she roared, her slim, five-foot-five-inch frame quivering with agitation. "The only carpet I need is a magic one—one that can fly me down these sixteen miles separating us and let me get close to you!"

Andy's brow furrowed into lines of concern. "You're really upset, aren't you?" he asked.

"Yes, I'm upset," Carrie said, staring around the room. "Look at us! We've been married only two months, and we're sitting so far apart we'd lose sight of each other if a fog set in."

Andrew broke into an outright grin. "Carrie, you are given to hyperbole. Are you aware of that?"

"There you go again," she wailed, slapping her forehead in exasperation. "Hyperbole! Why don't you just say I exaggerate?"

A wicked smirk teased one corner of Andrew's firm but sensual lips. "Because I'm a college professor, my dear, and I have to keep up appearances."

"With me?" she howled, shooting up from her chair and hurrying across the room to throw her arms around her husband's neck. "Andrew Everest," she whispered, "do you know what I'd like to be able to do with you every morning at breakfast?"

He caught her in his arms and held her firmly in his lap. "What?" he murmured, his lips exploring the creamy surface of her neck.

Carrie felt those now familiar liquid quiverings shiver through her. "This," she whispered, nibbling on his earlobe. "And this . . ." She let her arms circle his strong neck and found his lips with hers, kissing him with all the sweet ardor soaring inside her.

"Mmm," he crooned when the kiss ended. "I like it."

She stared into his wonderful gray eyes. "Oh, darling, I like it, too." Her mouth softened into a smile as she rested her head against his strong shoulder. "This is what I want every morning, Andrew. Not sixteen feet of mahogany separating us."

He frowned. "But, honey, three generations of Everests have sat at this table every morning in exactly these chairs. My grandfather and grandmother, then my father and mother, and now you and me. For years and years Alma has automatically set the table this way. It's become an Everest tradition, Carrie." He looked around the gracious room, his gaze settling on the portrait of his grandfather that hung over the fireplace mantel. "If we changed it now, grandfather would probably roll over in his grave."

Carrie's gaze softened as she nodded. "Yes, honey, but we'd be beginning a tradition of our own." She touched his strong chin gently, love glowing within her. "Andrew, tradition is wonderful when it fulfills a purpose," she said quietly. "But I don't want to wake up some day forty years from now and realize that all we did was relive your grandparents' and parents' lives. We've got our own lives to live, darling." She smiled. "I wouldn't mind your burying yourself in *The Wall Street Journal* and the Asquith *Express* every morning as long as I was close enough to burrow underneath them and kiss you soundly when I got the whim."

Andrew hesitated, his eyes still on the portrait of his grandfather. Then he relented. "Okay. We'll have Alma set you a place next to mine starting tomorrow."

Carrie sat up straighter and shook her head. "Uh-uh."

Andrew stared at her. "What do you mean, 'uh-uh'?" he asked slowly.

She raised her chin stubbornly and looked down the length of her pert nose at him. "I mean we don't have to have breakfast in this formal room at all. I'd like to eat in that darling little porch just off the kitchen."

He stared at her, wondering how well he really knew this petite bit of dynamite who was now his wife. Sometimes she seemed to be an alien being, frequently coming up with new notions that astounded him. He knew that if he were a man given to introspection, he might try to puzzle out exactly what it was about Carrie that was so enticing, so very attractive. But he didn't especially care to dissect his relationship with his wonderful new wife; he simply wanted to enjoy it.

He guessed he was even changing because of Carrie, but he hadn't analyzed that either. They were subtle, almost undetectable, changes on the surface, but he suspected that somewhere deep inside, where his heart and soul lived, monumental elements were shifting, like great mountains moving under the force of an earthquake. Still, he didn't want to examine those changes too closely. Perhaps, he reflected, it was slightly frightening.

He heaved an exaggerated sigh and grinned at her. "The breakfast porch, is it? What will it be next? All new furniture? A new house, perhaps?"

She grinned, shaking her head while circling his neck with her arms. Leaning down, she rubbed her nose against his. "Uh-uh," she murmured. "Just the breakfast porch in the morning."

"Oh, sure," he teased, laughing as he hugged her. "I know you, Carrie Emerson Everest. You're a regular revolutionary. You'll be opening the house to wayward kids one of these days, or starting a soup kitchen, or using the pool in the summer as a haven for those cute little threatened baby seals."

Carrie drew back, her green eyes snapping with a combination of laughter and indignation. "And what would be wrong with using the Everest pool to save endangered seals?" she asked threateningly.

Andrew laughed, holding up his hands as if to ward off her attack. "Nothing! Your revolutionary spirit is already infecting me. Next thing you know, I'll be joining you in your protests. What is it this month? Acid rain?"

Carrie straightened her shoulders, trying for a sense of stature. "Fighting the pollution that's producing acid rain is an ongoing project. When will you learn that you can't stop fighting a worthwhile battle until the cause is won irrevocably?"

He reached out and ruffled her tousled mop of

black curls. "My little Marxist," he said affectionately.

"Marxist!" Carrie broke into astonished laughter.
"Me? Can't you just picture me in Russia? I'd be
banished to Siberia for my revolutionary zeal." She
threw her arms around her husband's neck and kissed
him soundly. "Oh, Andrew, haven't you realized yet
that I'm just a red-blooded American woman?"

He grinned. "I realized that the moment I met you.
There I was, standing in your bookstore with a stack
of books in my arms, and there you were, halfway
up a ladder, trying to get some ancient tome for some
little old gray-haired lady." His gray eyes sparkled as
he reminisced. "I remember it well. You were wearing
a skirt—some short cotton thing, I think. Navy blue.
And flat-heeled navy canvas espadrilles. And your
legs..." He sighed in pretended ecstasy. "It was your
legs that did it. I took one look at them and knew you
were as red-blooded and as womanly as they come.
I fell in love with you right there, on the spot."

Carrie laughed, taking up the narrative. "And I,
climbing down from my perch on the ladder, turned
to find this extraordinarily handsome, distinguished
professorial type staring at me." She grinned as she
ran her finger lightly over his firm, square chin. "I
swear to goodness, your mouth was hanging open. I
wanted to tell you to close it or you'd let in flies."

"But did you? No. You smiled sweetly at that little
old lady and fussed over her for what seemed like
fifteen more minutes—"

"And in reality was no more than two minutes,"
she interrupted smoothly.

"—and you finally turned to me," he continued,
barely blinking an eye at her interruption. "That's

when I knew it was all over for me. My bachelor days were at an end. Those green eyes, laughing at me, taunting me, telling me you knew all about the lascivious thoughts that were tumbling about in my gray matter—"

"And approved of them highly," Carrie finished. "There's not a thing in the world wrong with thoughts like that when two people are as attracted to each other as we were, from the moment we met." She shook her head disparagingly. "You and your proper Everest upbringing. Who knows how long it might have taken you to ask me out if I hadn't asked you out first?"

"Yes, and if I remember correctly, you asked me to marry you, too. I was properly shocked at your forwardness."

She giggled. "And you answered surprisingly fast in the affirmative, if I remember correctly."

Andrew grinned his wonderful crooked grin. "Well, I may be reserved, honey, but I'm no fool."

Carrie lowered her eyes, her laughter suddenly extinguished. "Everyone at the university thought you were," she said, her voice low and hesitant.

Andrew cocked his head to study his wife's expression. She had a supremely open face, a face that revealed all her thoughts, all her fears. She wasn't one to hide behind a polite facade or to beam outwardly while inside she was crying. She showed her feelings, whatever they were—joy, anger, fear, astonishment, love—and it was one of the many things he loved about her. He, who had been raised in a household devoid of expressions of emotion, found Carrie irresistibly appealing.

But now he saw the hesitation in her face, the faint

trepidation. She was asking for reassurance.

He reached out and gently lifted her chin with his fingers. "Hey," he murmured, "what's going on with Ms. Carrie Emerson Everest, the happiest lady on the block? Is that a cloud I see blocking out her sunshine?"

Carrie looked up swiftly, breaking into a radiant grin. Impulsively she put her arms around him and hugged him tightly. "Oh, Andrew," she sighed, "I love you so much. Sometimes I can't believe we're really married. It all happened so quickly. We met in September and were married just before Christmas. Is it any wonder I sometimes get afraid?"

"Afraid of what?" he asked gently, stroking her curls, cradling her slim body in his.

She shook her head. "Oh, it's just that I know we've shocked all your friends. I'm not quite sure why . . ." She trailed off, lifting questioning green eyes to his reassuring gray ones.

"Because, I suppose, my lady, you're so damnably adorable. Everyone must be wondering what you saw in this staid, stuffy old professor from the most conservative university in the States."

"You?" she asked. "Staid?" She threw her head back and laughed. "Stuffy? Would that they all could see you in the bedroom, Herr Professor! They'd soon see what this 'adorable' lady saw in you."

He grinned, one corner of his firmly etched lips curving wryly as he slid a hand around the nape of her neck and began to massage it gently. "You mean I satisfy you?" he asked, laughing softly.

"Satisfy me!" Carrie shot bolt upright and placed her hands on his shoulders, looking deeply into his laughing gray eyes. "Andrew Everest," she said solemnly, "you are hell on wheels in the bedroom. Satisfy me? You satiate me! You make me want you morning, noon, and night. When I'm at the bookstore I find myself getting all turned on just thinking about you." She rubbed her cheek against his smoothly shaven one. "Oh, darling, what an absurd question. Did you ever doubt you satisfied me?"

"Well, come to think of it, you *do* moan a lot."

She slugged him playfully, then hugged him, laughing.

"Well," he said, "the feeling's mutual, Caroline. Do you know that I spent the entire time during the meeting of the history department yesterday afternoon just thinking about you? I was so carried away that when Dr. Hopewell, our illustrious department chairman, asked me a question, I couldn't answer. I hadn't even heard the question."

Carrie giggled. "Must have been rather embarrassing."

"Oh, I just cleared my throat a few times and fussed with my pipe, and everyone assumed I was thinking deep, scholarly thoughts."

"Deceiver," Carrie said, tweaking his nose. "If only they knew."

Andrew smiled thoughtfully. "It's a funny thing, Carrie, but I never used to be like this. Until I met you, there wasn't a woman on this earth who was capable of capturing my thoughts during a department meeting. I was as solemn and pompous as the rest of them, sitting there in my tweeds with my pipe and horn-rimmed glasses, thinking great, lofty thoughts." He grinned. "Now all I think about is getting you into bed."

Carrie's smile was thoughtful. "Does that bother you? Am I too much of a nuisance?"

"Nuisance! Whoever called you a nuisance?" He grasped her arms and held her steady as he looked into her questioning eyes. "If you're a nuisance, Carrie, then that's exactly what I've been needing all my life." He shook his head. "Oh, no, Carrie darling, don't ever go thinking you're a nuisance. I love you— everything about you. Don't ever change."

She smiled, then leaned and kissed him gently on the lips. "Oh, Andrew, what do you say we leave this place and ascend to the bedroom, therein to play all day?"

He laughed and shook his head, helping her to rise and then sliding his chair back. "Tempting as the offer is, I must refuse. I've got an eight-o'clock class." He looked at the slim, expensive gold watch that circled his strong wrist. "Dammit, I'll be late. All this talk has set me back ten minutes."

Carrie laughed, reaching up to smooth his hair and straighten his tie. "Whatever will the Asquith community say? Andrew Everest ten minutes off schedule? It must be due to that upstart wife of his!"

"Hmm," he said. "The talk will spread like wildfire. If I catch the students giggling in class, I'll know what they're thinking."

Carrie rose up on tiptoe and kissed him lingeringly. "Take care, Andrew," she whispered against his lips. "Don't let any of those blond coeds get to you."

"My taste doesn't run to blond coeds," he said, leaning over to pick up his briefcase from beside his chair. When he straightened, he bestowed a final kiss on Carrie's nose. "If it did, I'd have been caught and married long ago."

He seemed about to walk out when he turned back and reached out, dragging Carrie into his embrace.

His lips scorched hers. "My taste, Mrs. Everest," he said, his voice low and vibrating with emotion, "runs to semi-short, tousle-headed moppets with green eyes who do indecent things to their husbands in their husbands' ancestral homes."

She arched an eyebrow. "Indecent? What have I done that's indecent?"

"You've made me wish heartily that I didn't have an eight-o'clock class to get to. You've overturned a habit of a hundred years' standing by talking me into eating on the breakfast porch, which has remained unused ever since the architect who redid the kitchen talked my mother into having it built on. And those are just for starters."

Carrie peered up at him. "So you think it's indecent that you'd rather be in bed with me than teaching a class, do you?"

His eyes flickered toward the portrait of his staid grandfather. *"He'd* think so."

"But do you?" Carrie asked softly.

He stared down at her, then shook his head. "No. I think every time we make love, no matter when or where or how, it's the most beautiful thing on earth." His eyes traveled once again to the portrait. He studied it solemnly before he spoke. "They didn't discuss sex openly," he said musingly. "But I got the feeling that both my parents and grandparents considered it a necessary evil. Not surprisingly, each couple had only one child: Grandfather and Grandmother had my father, and my parents had me." He looked back at Carrie and grinned. "Well, if we're going to start some new Everest traditions, let's add one more. Let's have a dozen kids."

"A dozen? Isn't that going a bit far?"

He leered at her. "Think of all the fun we'll have. Someone we can tell little Andrew that he was conceived in the study, and little Carrie that she was conceived on the porch swing, and little Bryan or Edward or Sidney that he was conceived in the backyard under a maple tree—"

"Whoa!" Carrie held up a hand. "Aren't any going to be conceived in a bed?"

He grinned as he walked toward the door, pausing to look back at her. "One or two," he said, winking. Then he closed the door behind him.

Carrie felt a tide of warmth flow over her. Looking around the palatial room, she spotted the portrait of Edward Haynes Everest, her husband's grandfather.

"Well," she said, smiling with satisfaction. "Looks like I scored one today, Grandfather."

She looked around the room once more and mentally said good-bye. The month-long siege of the dining room had ended, and she was the victor. Bending to clear the table, she looked up at the portrait once again.

"That's one for me and none for you, Grandfather. From now on, I'll be keeping score."

— 2 —

"MRS. EVEREST, HOW many times have I told you, it's *my* job to clear the table!" Alma Jenkins stood with her hands on her stout hips, her gray head cocked sideways, her merry blue eyes flashing with good-natured indignation.

Carrie laughed as she deposited the delicate Wedg-wood onto the counter near the dishwasher. "And how many times have I asked you to call me Carrie?"

Alma shook her head, giving the impression of a baby elephant shaking water off its back. "That's just not done in this house, ma'am," she said, hurrying to scrape the remainder of scrambled eggs off the plates before Carrie could do so. "In this house the lady is called Mrs. Everest. I was just a young thing when I started working in this kitchen, and old Mrs. Everest—Mr. Andy's grandmother—was the lady then. Of course, Mr. Andy's mother lived here then, too." Alma efficiently deposited the dishes in a pile near the sink—no dishwasher would touch the sacred Everest Wedgwood—and turned to see Carrie absently rubbing her nose as she stared toward the door that led to the sun porch.

Carrie smiled at Alma. "What were they like,

Alma—the two Everest women?" She hesitated, glancing down. "I'm . . . I'm very different, aren't I?"

Alma smiled broadly. "Yes, ma'am, you are, but I'd say it's a change for the better. The other two Mrs. Everests were . . . well, they were *ladies,* ma'am." Abruptly, looking horrified, Alma held out a beseeching hand. "Not that *you're* not a lady, ma'am, except you're more . . . well, you know, down to earth. They were above it all. They kind of floated around the house in long dresses and gave formal teas and were involved in all the local charities, but I never saw them smile. Now, you . . ." Alma laughed heartily. "My goodness, ma'am, I just love to be here in the kitchen and hear you and Mr. Andy in the dining room. You *laugh,* Mrs. Everest. You laugh like you really mean it. They never did. If they laughed at all, it was a polite little sound, held back behind a hanky. Yes, ma'am, you're sure different, but I like it!"

Carrie smiled. "Then why don't you call me Carrie?" she asked softly. "You just admitted I'm not like those other two Everest women."

"Oh, ma'am, I just couldn't," Alma shook her head as she wiped her hands nervously on her voluminous apron. "No, it just wouldn't be right in this house."

"But you call my husband Mr. Andy."

"But that's because I was here when he was born. Seems natural to call him Mr. Andy."

"Then call me Miss Carrie."

Alma's eyes widened. "But you're a *Missus.*"

Carrie laughed helplessly. "Who cares? Please, Alma, do it for me. I'd appreciate it. I've never been one for formality."

Alma shook her head doubtfully. "I sure don't know how you and Mr. Andy ended up together." She looked up, round-eyed. "Not that you're not meant for each other! You are. Any fool can see how much you love each other." Alma frowned. "It's just that . . . well, I guess everyone thought Mr. Andy and Miss Constance Hopewell would end up together. Miss Constance— now, she's like the other Everest women." Then, realizing what she had just said, Alma turned away and began running hot water into a rubber dishpan. "Forgive me, Mrs. Everest. Sometimes I talk too much."

"I think you talk just right, Alma," Carrie said gently, smiling at her cook-housekeeper's broad back. Alma mumbled something like "Harrumph," and Carrie smiled and turned to go. She paused at the swinging door that led to the dining room. "Oh, by the way, Alma, Andrew and I have decided to eat our breakfast on the breakfast porch from now on. I just thought I'd let you know so you can put away the Wedgwood for breakfast and use something a bit less formal."

Shocked, Alma turned around, her bulky body moving like a whale's, and stared at her new mistress. "You *what?*" she asked, her loud voice booming in the quiet kitchen.

Carrie tried to suppress a giggle. The sight of Alma's expression of disbelief was too much. "We've decided to eat on the breakfast porch," Carrie repeated, as if it were of no importance. "I think that architect who redid the kitchen had a wonderful idea about adding on the breakfast room. I just can't understand why Andrew's mother never used that wonderful little porch. It's so cheery and sunny."

Alma shook her head, her jowls waggling. "She didn't eat there because it just isn't *done*, Mrs. Everest. That's why."

"But it *is*," Carrie insisted with a firm but gentle

smile. "Beginning tomorrow." She pushed open the
door, then looked back at the incredulous Alma. "Oh,
and Alma?"

"Yes, ma'am?"

"It's Carrie, not Mrs. Everest."

"Yes, Mrs. Everest."

Carrie planted her hands on her hips and waited.
Finally, Alma heaved a sigh of resignation and passed
a massive hand over her forehead. "Yes, Miss Carrie."

A beatific smile claimed Carrie's face. "See you.
Have a good day." Waving, she strutted from the
kitchen. Her day was a complete success, and it had
only just begun.

"Good morning, Dr. Everest."

"Good morning, Dr. Everest."

Andrew smiled absently at the two blond coeds,
their faces lit with flirtatious smiles, their blue eyes
momentarily shaded by fluttering lashes—a tech-
nique, he assumed with gentle amusement, they had
picked up by watching old Greta Garbo movies. He
had to keep himself from grinning as he remembered
Carrie's remark of just that morning—about watching
out for those blond coeds. His lips twitched at the
corners. He had taught at Asquith for six years, and
in all that time not a single coed had caught his eye.

He chuckled to himself as he strode toward the ivy-
covered building that bore the name of his grandfather.
Well, he supposed one or two had caught his eye in
the past six years, but they'd never held it for very
long. He had never questioned his unresponsiveness
to the young and often beautiful women who attended
Asquith, but he supposed vaguely that it was because
he had become immune. He'd been raised just off

campus, gone to an elite prep school, then entered Asquith and acquired three degrees in rapid succession: Bachelor of Arts, Master's, and finally Ph.D. Immediately thereafter he'd joined the faculty.

Asquith was, after all, in his blood. His grandfather had been chairman of the history department, his father had been chairman of the history department, and it was generally supposed that one day he, too, would become chairman of the department, a largely honorary post held by professors who possessed a keen sense of responsibility and loyalty to Asquith. His grandfather and father had. Andrew frowned as he jogged up the granite steps of Edward Haynes Everest Hall. Lately, though, he was beginning to wonder if he did.

Since he'd met Carrie last September, nothing much had seemed to matter as much as she did. He was endlessly fascinated by his wife. She was totally extraordinary—a completely new species of womanhood. She swore like a Marine when angered, drank whiskey neat, rode a ten-speed bike to her bookstore daily, and turned him to mush every time he looked at her.

He was still puzzling out the fascination she held for him when he was hailed by a deep, resounding male voice. Turning, Andrew spied Professor Lawrence Hopewell, current chairman of the history department, approaching. He was a tall, gray-haired, distinguished-looking man, given to rough English tweeds, corduroy trousers, and a briar pipe. He had an air of abstraction about him, as if he were lost in intellectual thought. Andrew suspected it was a mannerism; Larry was probably thinking about the latest

James Bond thriller he had hidden in his office.

"Morning, Larry," Andrew said, falling into step beside his older colleague. Lawrence Hopewell was the age Andrew's father would have been, and had taken over the chairmanship when the elder Everest died of cancer at the young age of fifty-two. Andrew's mother had passed away a year later. Since then Larry had taken a paternal attitude toward Andrew, joking that he would hold the chairmanship until Andrew was ready to assume it.

Larry put a fatherly hand on Andrew's shoulder, pulling him out of the stream of traffic in the hall and biting on his pipe as he spoke. "You'll be coming up for tenure this term, you know."

Andrew nodded, feeling an absurd twist of discomfort in his gut. Tenure. The ultimate goal in academia. He supposed it was virtually assured for him; his background, after all, should make him a shoo-in. Besides, he had written the required papers and had been published in professional journals with good credentials. But somehow it had never seemed to matter enough to him. His heart hadn't been in it.

After meeting Carrie, he had joked that he felt as if he had been programmed, much the way a young prince born in England must feel—tutored from birth to take his appointed place in life, with no way out save abdication.

Andrew glanced at Larry, who was gazing vaguely at the ceiling, his head wreathed in pipe smoke, his eyes properly reflective and professorial.

"Yes," Larry said, nodding, "coming up for tenure."

The older man's eyes shifted for a second toward

Andrew, then shifted away uneasily. "There could be trouble this year, you realize."

"Trouble?"

"Women!" Lawrence Hopewell sneered, puffing furiously on his pipe. "Making a row in some of the other departments that they're not getting tenure as easily as the men." Larry laughed derisively. "Small wonder! They're just not as qualified. Harvard and the rest can make spectacles of themselves by giving women tenure, but Asquith will stick to its standards."

Andrew looked down at his shoes, a quick movement designed to hide his sudden grin. At Asquith there was an old saying: First there was Asquith, and trailing along afterward were the Ivy League schools. An Asquith alumnus disdained the so-called "lesser Ivy League colleges," claiming that Asquith was kin only to the great Cambridge and Oxford in England. Nothing in the United States could touch Asquith for intellectual purity. It was a particular kind of snobbishness that infuriated Carrie, and Andrew wanted to laugh out loud at the thought of how she would react to Larry's statement. Carrie was big on women's lib—or feminism, as she called it.

"Well," said Andrew equably, "there are some damned smart women here at Asquith. I don't think we'd lose out by granting them tenure."

"Horse feathers!" Larry scoffed, taking his pipe from his mouth and peering at Andrew through the haze of smoke. "You surely can't mean that." Then his expression altered subtly. "Oh. Oh, yes, I see. It's that little wife of yours, I suppose."

"My 'little wife'?" Andrew asked, a dangerous edge to his voice.

Larry waved his pipe absently. "Yes, yes, yes,

what's her name? Cassie? Candy? Ah, yes. Carrie."
Larry bit down on his pipe again and blew out a
threatening stream of smoke. "Damned strange of you,
Andy, to marry that little bit of a thing." He leaned
forward and whispered conspiratorially. "Bed her if
you must, Andy, but marry her?" He shook his head
disapprovingly. "You made a mistake there, Andy,
but you'll come around. You'll see. Divorce isn't as
much frowned on these days as it once was. There's
still time to remedy this misjudgment of yours."

Andrew gave Lawrence Hopewell a glacial gray
stare. "And whom would you have me marry, Larry?"

Larry laughed heartily. "Good Lord, Andy do I
have to tell you? Connie's been waiting for you for
years." Larry's eyes brightened. "Wonderful girl, my
daughter. Wonderful. Exquisite beauty, eh, Andy?
Like the *Mona Lisa*, don't you think? Calm, somewhat
wistful." Larry sighed, expelling more smoke. "Ah,
well, the wistfulness is over you, you young pup. But
you'll come around."

He clapped Andrew on the back and laughed heartily. "Yes, you just wait. You'll see your error and be
divorced within a year. The newness will wear off . . ."
Larry's eyes took on a sly gleam. "The lust will wane.
Then you'll get a quiet divorce and get back on track."
He grinned wolfishly and laughed his hearty laugh
again. "Back on the tenure track!" he joked. Then,
waving his pipe absently, he was off down the hall,
his shoulders slumping inside his British tweed jacket,
blue pipe smoke trailing behind him like a banner.

For a moment, watching Larry walk away, Andrew
felt an absurd desire to run after him, swing him
around by the shoulder, and plant a fist in his pompous
face. Mistake, was it? Lust, eh? His face reddening

with anger, Andrew strode toward the stairs and took them two at a time, shouldering past the dawdling students without so much as an "Excuse me."

Once in his office, he shoved his briefcase onto his littered desk and stepped over to the window. He leaned on the sill and looked out. Students littered the snow-covered campus like ants on an anthill. The sun shone on the ice-encrusted trees and sent blinding flashes of light into the chill February air.

February first. Despite his anger, Andrew felt his lips twitch in remembrance. February first, and he and Carrie had instituted a new Everest tradition. Then his smile faded as he recalled Larry Hopewell's words. Hostility flickered within him, and his hands tightened into fists.

Pushing himself away from the window, he walked back to his desk and stood looking down at the pile of papers on it. For some reason he couldn't summon up the desire to sit down and begin preparing for class. For some reason he wanted to chuck it all, the whole damned schedule, and walk down to Carrie's store, where a fireplace burned merrily and patrons loitered for hours, sipping coffee, tea, or hot chocolate, alternately talking with Carrie or browsing through the books. He wanted to be with Carrie, dammit. He wanted to be with Carrie...

Promptly at six o'clock Carrie locked the door to her store, Book Ends, and turned the sign so that the CLOSED side faced outward. She hurried to the phone and called home. The second ring produced an answer.

"Andrew?" she said happily. "Hi."

"Will you be home soon, dumpling?" he asked.

Carrie made a face. "You've forgotten again. It's Wednesday. You know I don't come right home on Wednesdays."

He groaned. "Ah, yes. The famous Women's Wednesdays."

"Darling, you know how important this group is for me," Carrie said softly. "And not only for me, but for all the women. We're a...a..." Carrie searched for a new word to describe their group. *Network* sounded so dry. An informal support group was what it was, in essence. "It's just very important to all of us that we meet. We think alike. We need each other; we get sustenance from each other."

"You can get all the sustenance you need from me," Andrew said grumpily.

Carrie grinned. "You're jealous of a bunch of women."

"Oh, for crying out loud, I'm *not* jealous!"

"You are!" Carrie cried, delighted. "You really are! Why, I think that's marvelous. Totally out of character."

"And what makes that so marvelous?" Andrew asked carefully.

"Oh, darling, because you're usually so logical and unemotional! This is a great breakthrough. We'll celebrate when I get home." She lowered her voice to a seductive whisper. "Turn down the lights and put a bottle of champagne on ice. I'm sure we can think of something special to do after we drink it..."

Andrew groaned. "Carrie, your voice alone is turning me on."

She nodded, feeling strangely giddy. "Yes. All of a sudden I wish it weren't Wednesday," she said, her voice throaty.

"So skip the meeting," he said, hope rising in his voice.

She shook her head. "Can't. The meeting is *here*, after all. I've got to be here for the other women, and I've got to be here for me, too. It's important."

"More important than coming home to your love-starved husband?"

She bit her lower lip and toyed with the telephone wire.

"Well?" he prompted. "Is it more important than I?"

"No, it's not *more* important than you. It's *as* important as you, though, in its own way."

She heard him chuckle, and relief flooded through her. He understood. It was wonderful knowing she had her husband's support and understanding about something that mattered so much to her.

"Okay," he said, "you meet with that group of hens, and I'll keep the home fires burning. When you've exhausted your vocal chords, pedal on home and we'll share a drink by a cozy fire in the study."

"And then?" she asked, lowering her voice to a husky murmur.

"And then," he answered, his voice sending shivers of anticipation over her skin, "we'll let matters take care of themselves."

"Meaning . . . ?"

He chuckled again. "Meaning we'll make up for any time lost at your women's Wednesday meeting."

Carrie laughed, said good-bye, and hung up. She got a carton of yogurt from the small refrigerator in her office and wandered toward the fireplace at the back of the store. Pulling up an antique bow-backed Windsor chair, she plopped into it and propped her feet on the hearth, feeling the warmth seep into her leather boots. She dipped her spoon into her yogurt and stared into the flames while waiting for the women to arrive.

There were twelve of them now, although the number fluctuated. Sometimes as few as four showed up; sometimes they all gathered around the crackling fireplace in winter or out on the deck at the back of the store in the summer and spring. And they'd talk, good old-fashioned woman talk. The kind of talk you couldn't always share with a man. The kind of talk you indulged in with close friends, with people you trusted.

And they did trust each other. They'd been through a lot in the past eight or nine months they'd been meeting: separations, a divorce, her own marriage, the death of a father, the death of a child, the loss of a job, the start of a first job, and more. Oh, they'd shared it all, laughing and yelling and talking full tilt, gesturing, hugging, supporting, crying. Sometimes they polished off a bottle or two of wine. At other times they had coffee or tea or hot chocolate.

She wondered what kind of night it would turn out to be tonight—tea, coffee, hot chocolate, or wine?

"Wine, dammit!" Louise Henderson snapped, dropping into a chair.

"Uh-oh," Carrie said sympathetically as she walked back toward her office to get a bottle of chilled Chablis. "That bad, eh?"

"Worse," Louise called after her. When Carrie returned, Louise held out her glass and let Carrie fill it to the top, then drank half of it in one gulp.

Fascinated, Carrie edged into her chair, looking

around at the six other women assembled. "Well, I guess this is going to be Louise's night."

Everyone laughed and nodded, and there was a general tumble of conversation as they all got more comfortable. Carrie eyed each of them, feeling a special warmth. There was Mary Jackson, fifty years old, recently widowed, and wondering where her life was going; Ceil Feline, twenty-six and married, stuck in her house all day with three toddlers; Muffie Horowitz, thirty-eight and struggling with a recent mastectomy; Susan Cummings, thirty-two and recently separated, out on her own and worrying over finances for the first time in her life; Allison Sterling, forty-three, a former Miss America who now operated a beauty salon; and Paige Carter, sixty-five, an elegant, wealthy woman whose husband had recently retired from the diplomatic corps. Only months before, Paige had lost her only son in an automobile accident, and the pain of it was still evident in her eloquent blue eyes.

But now all eyes were on Louise Henderson, at thirty-nine an assistant professor of English at Asquith. She was an attractive brunette with carefully coiffed hair and neat makeup. She wore nicely tailored clothes and kept in shape by skiing in the winter and swimming in the summer. She was intelligent, ambitious, and clearly very, very angry.

"Okay," Carrie said, settling back in her chair and cupping her wineglass in her hands. "What gives?"

Louise set her glass down and dug in her pocketbook for a cigarette. They all watched as she lit it, her hands trembling. She let out a huge breath and emitted a stream of smoke.

"It's Asquith," she said tightly. "Staid, conservative, uptight Asquith University. The domain of the scholarly, dignified, erudite, and utterly prejudiced *male!*" She roared the last word, almost making the exposed beams in the rustic store rattle.

"Hmm," Carrie said softly. "Asquith. Care to tell us what exactly about the males at Asquith is upsetting you so? Has one made a pass at you? Sexual harassment—that kind of stuff?"

Louise grimaced and waved a hand. "Hell, no. If one of those buzzards did, I'd deck him. No, it's worse. Much worse. It's tenure time."

"Care to elaborate?" Susan Cummings gently prompted.

Louise took another drag on her cigarette. Suddenly the fire left her eyes and voice and she looked utterly resigned, drained of all emotion. She tipped back her head and gazed up at the rafters. "Let me tell you about tenure. You get a Ph.D. at a good school—mine was from Yale—and then you land a job as an assistant professor. You teach five years at the very least, do lots of research, publish some papers—maybe a book—and you come up, eventually, for tenure. Job security, in other words," she elaborated. "If you're nominated and approved for tenure after all that other stuff, your position is yours for as long as you want it—provided you don't do something outrageous and get yourself expelled from the university. If you don't get tenure, you're allowed a year to secure another teaching position and start over somewhere else."

She paused and puffed on her cigarette. "Me, I got a late start: didn't finish my Ph.D. until I was thirty-two. So here I am, seven years later, having taught English at Asquith for six years, and I'm coming up for tenure." Her brown eyes scanned the group of women, who hung on her every word. "And you know what's going to happen?"

No one spoke, and Louise's gaze came to rest on Carrie. She sighed heavily, stubbed out her cigarette, struggled to light another, then pretended that the smoke had gotten into her eyes when she began to blink back tears. "You know what's going to happen?" she asked, her voice plaintive.

Hunched forward, sending out all the empathy she could muster, Carrie shook her head. "No, Louise," she said softly, benevolently. "What's going to happen?"

Louise tightened her lips and took another deep breath. "I won't get it, dammit—that's what's going to happen. I won't get it."

Carrie stared at her, seeing the misery, anger, and disillusionment in her face. "But how do you know?" she asked. "You're just nervous, Louise."

Louise shook her head, looking once more around the semicircle of women. "No," she said finally. "You want to know why I won't get tenure?" She didn't wait for an answer. She leaned forward and enunciated every word perfectly. "I won't get tenure at Asquith," she said quietly, "simply because I am a woman."

3

CARRIE BENT TO stir the dying embers, poking at the remains of a charred log in the fireplace. Then she went from window to window, making sure each was locked and fastening the wooden shutters across each for the night. Her forehead was creased in a thoughtful frown as she pulled on her coat and slid her hands into gloves. Then she threw her shoulder bag over her arm, locked the front door of Book Ends, and bent to unlock the chain that fastened her bicycle to a lamp post.

A moment later she was on the bike, her skirt flaring around her legs, her booted feet flying in small circles as she pedaled energetically. Her tires squished through the slush coating the quiet, lamplit streets, sending up a fine spray of muddy snow that caught the moon's dim rays and turned it to muted silver in the night.

She savored the wind rushing against her reddening cheeks and blowing her short curls into disarray. As she rounded the corner into her street her heart lurched: She spied the familiar figure of her husband, his hands thrust into his jacket pockets, his head thrown back against the bitter wind, standing at the entrance to their driveway, waiting for her. She slowed to make the turn into the driveway and skidded to a stop, her joy etched on her face as she drank in the sight of him.

"Give you a lift, fella?"

He grinned and reached out to tweak her red nose. "Naw, lady, that's okay. I'm waiting for my wife."

Carrie threw him a grin and began to pedal the bicycle slowly as Andrew strolled by her side, their destination the three-car garage at the end of the driveway.

"So how was the famous Woman's Wednesday meeting?" he asked, reaching down to pick up a piece of ice and toss it in a bright arc across the wide expanse of lawn. They heard it land on the crusty surface of the glittering snow, and Andrew pulled open the garage door as Carrie dismounted the bike.

She wrinkled her nose as she guided the bike past Andrew and pushed the kickstand into position. "Disturbing," she said, turning to him. "You know Louise Henderson, don't you?"

Andrew's eyes took on the thoughtful glaze Carrie had come to know; it meant he was scanning his brain for a name, date, or place, much as a computer scans its data bank.

"Henderson," he said finally. "Yeah. English department. Good instructor. The kids like her. Specializes in modern poetry."

He slid the door shut, padlocked it, and took Carrie's arm in his as they fell into step beside each other and made for the house. He turned his head and read the disquiet on his wife's face. "Why?" he asked quietly. "Was she at the meeting?"

"Actually, she dominated the meeting." Carrie

smiled. "I don't mean that the way it sounds. You see, it's all very informal, but each time we meet it seems it's another woman's turn to take the floor and air her problems. Tonight it was Louise's." She hesitated, climbing the brick steps that led to the back door. "She's coming up for tenure."

Andrew opened the door and motioned for Carrie to enter, then followed her into the welcoming warmth of the kitchen. "As a matter of fact, so am I. Hopewell brought it up this morning."

Carrie eyed her husband. "But you'll get it, won't you?"

"No reason to suppose I won't," he said, grinning, and began to unbutton her coat. When the last button was undone he slid his hands inside and pulled her forward, leaning his chilled cheek against her own.

"Brrr!" she cried, pulling away. "I'll make hot chocolate. Then, after you've held the mug for ten minutes or so, you can hold me."

He took their coats and hung them in the back closet, then sat down at the table in the breakfast porch and watched Carrie move briskly about the kitchen, making hot chocolate as efficiently as she did everything else. He watched her approach him, appreciating the lithe feminine lines beneath her clothing—the saucy upthrust of her small breasts, the mere suggestion of a wiggle in her slim hips, the firm, rounded outline of her delicious rump. When she set his mug on the table, he reached out and pulled her into his embrace, separating his legs so he could pull her into the V and hold her by her hips.

She smiled down into his face as her hands slid down onto his broad shoulders. She lowered her head to kiss him lingeringly.

"Mmmm," he murmured, his breath mingling with hers before his tongue slid forward to savor the moist honey of her lips. He heard her ragged breath and felt her slide closer, resting her trim rear end on one powerful thigh as she twined her arms around his neck. He ran his hands up her back and broke off the kiss to bury his head in the sweet curve where her creamy neck met her even creamier shoulders.

"I never get enough of you," he said hoarsely. "I want you incessantly. Is this becoming for a thirty-four-year-old history professor?"

She raised her head and grinned, tracing her forefinger along the devastating curve of his underlip. "Very becoming," she whispered, her gaze rising slowly from his lips to his gray eyes. She smiled impishly. "You're like the defrocked priest who discovers the joys of women. You'll settle down one of these years"—she laughed softly—"although I'm perfectly content to put up with this aberrant behavior from my own particular Asquith professor."

He slid his now warm hands under her sweater and with one movement unclipped her bra and cupped her tiny breasts in his strong hands. Letting his thumbs manipulate her nipples, he delighted in his power to make her respond so pleasingly. The pink buds burgeoned under his seeking thumbs, growing hard under his insistent touch, and he felt a familiar tug in his groin, the tightening that signaled his own arousal. He was gratified when Carrie pulled her sweater over her head and let it fall to the floor, but it was with reluctance that he removed his hands momentarily from her breasts, letting her lacy bra slide forward over her arms and in rumpled abandon next to her sweater.

Then his hands returned to their sweet treasure, his gaze feasting on the hardened nipples, at the soft, creamy slopes of her chest, which filled his palms and heated his blood to the point of mindless passion. With a low growl he picked her up and walked swiftly through the kitchen, shouldering his way through the swinging door that led to the hallway, heading for the study, where a fire burned cheerily in the grate. He walked across the thick luxuriance of the Oriental carpet and laid her down on the velvet sofa that faced the fireplace, reaching out to find a chintz-covered pillow to tuck under her head. Then he knelt in front of the couch and lowered his lips to her breasts in quiet homage.

He heard her quickening breath with a kind of exultation. He felt her hands grip his head, tangling in his dark hair as she strove to hold his lips against her breasts and let his tongue have its way. But the more he sucked and stroked her swollen buds with his tongue, the more he wanted. His hands wandered lower, seeking the soft, silken texture of her pantyhose, remembering with delight how he had stripped off those pantyhose so often in the past to expose the soft cream of her thighs to his touch.

He chuckled when he realized she was too excited to endure his slow ministrations. She pushed herself into a sitting position and began tearing off her clothes until, naked, clothed only in the glow from the fireplace, she lay back and smothered a gasp of pure pleasure as he laid his head on her stomach and let his hand glide sensuously from her knees to her thighs. He paused only briefly, then flattened his palm over the soft, down-covered mound of her womanhood. While his hand made tantalizing circles, he turned his lips to her flat stomach and traced fiery lines with his tongue across the ivory of her abdomen.

He heard her moan softly and whisper his name in a kind of entreaty. Again he felt the exultation, the sheer joy, that he had this wonderful power to arouse her—she who aroused him with merely a soft glance. He knew it was a kind of miracle, a gift of the gods to him whose life had once seemed so sterile, so remote from earthly passions, so entangled in scholarly pursuits.

Suddenly those so-called lofty pursuits held no thrall. A far more enticing need had swelled within him—the need to hold and merge with this woman, his wife, to delve so deeply into her that he became one with her. More than once he had found himself marveling at the beautiful conjunction of their bodies. Their mating always produced such incredible beauty, such unearthly bliss, an altered state of consciousness that seized them and sent them hurtling into the heavens, to drift, bedazzled, among the stars, to become, for fierce, golden, precious moments, like gods themselves.

He raised his head and looked into her drowsy green eyes, reaching out with infinite tenderness to caress her cheek.

"My God, I love you," he whispered. "It's as if I walked in darkness all my life until you brought me light and warmth." He dropped adoring lips to her breasts once again. "Oh, Carrie," he breathed, "I love you so very, very much."

Her green eyes filled with tears, and she caressed his hair, smoothing it back from his temples. She stroked his powerful shoulder, her hands moving ceaselessly, every inch of his body a drug she was addicted to.

"Andrew," she murmured. "Let me undress you."

But he shook his head impatiently and began tearing at the buttons of his shirt, yanking them apart to expose the tangle of hair on his chest. He shucked off his shirt, then stood, making short work of kicking off his shoes, unbuckling his belt, unzipping his fly, and shoving his trousers and briefs over his lean male hips and down the powerful thighs and calves. Naked, he settled down beside her on the couch, his hands finding the slim indentation of her waist, that soft hollow between the swell of breasts and hips, as his eyes adored her.

And it was finally her turn to let her hands rove his beloved body, letting them drift over the solid, hair-covered expanse of his muscled chest, down his flat, rippling midriff to his even flatter belly, so firm, so unlike her own, to the hard appendage that would soon fill her. How soft the skin on it! How delicate, to contain so much seething power!

She heard his ragged breathing, felt his lips on her neck, felt his hands running up and down her back, settling here on a rounded hip, there on the twin globes of her rump, cupping them and pulling her toward his ripe manhood so that it lay, throbbing with need, against her stomach, causing her breath to catch in her throat.

She lifted her thigh, settled it over his, and inched her pelvis forward, guiding his manhood to her yearning center. Facing each other, eyes wide and staring into each other's soul, they joined. She shuddered at the penetration, wrapped her arms around his neck, and closed her eyes, settling her head into the powerful curve of his shoulder and neck and moving her body in time with his deep thrusts. With every stroke she felt the frenzy mount, felt the sweet assault on her senses, felt herself opening and flowering, felt his hardness enter her deeper and deeper, filling her.

She caught her lip in her teeth to smother a cry of ecstasy, and she heard him murmur against her neck, "Don't hold it back, my darling. Let it come. Shout it. I want to hear your joy."

And he pushed into her with heightening urgency, as if driven by some demon need. Her head rolled back as she felt his lips plunder the sensitive flesh of her neck; felt his rigid manhood thrust ever deeper; felt herself open in liquid, heated response; felt the soft, slow lifting toward the heavens; felt the world fall away beneath her as she drifted toward the stars. She dug her fingertips into his broad, powerful back and began to gasp, knowing it was coming, as surely and inevitably as the sun would rise in the East. Deep in her body the vibrations began, like distant thunder, and all the time Andrew stroked, stroked, driving her farther and farther into the welcoming blackness, the oblivion, the tiny death, as the French called it.

And then she felt Andrew's muscles bunch up, felt his arms tighten around her, and she knew he, too, was approaching it. They clung to each other, merging, withdrawing, merging, in a rhythm evocative of waves washing against the shore. Suddenly the blackness rolled, and the thunder rumbled up from deep within them. They clutched each other, and a golden cascade of sweet release broke over them in blinding radiance. Their cries shattered the quiet in the dimly lit room, and they soared into the heavens, where they remained suspended, wrapped in each other's arms, before slowly drifting back to earth, their breathing ragged, their bodies damp.

They lay side by side, at peace, until the coolness of the room began to penetrate their halo of inner warmth. Carrie snuggled up against Andrew.

"Cold?" he asked, angling his head to look into her eyes.

"A little."

He got up, found an afghan, and settled it over them, then laid back and burrowed one strong arm under her neck and held her close.

Ever so slowly, mundane cares and concerns returned. Andrew remembered his conversation with Larry Hopewell that morning. Carrie frowned as she went over Louise Henderson's words, spoken only a few hours earlier.

"Andrew?"

"Hmm?"

"Is it difficult for women to get tenure at Asquith?"

He shrugged. "I've never really thought about it." He laughed. "I spoke with old Hopewell this morning. If he's any indication, it definitely is. Why?"

"I was remembering what Louise Henderson said tonight. She quoted some dreadful statistics. She said that at one university here in Connecticut, a study was done by the American Association of University Professors, and it found that twenty-one percent of female professors were denied merit increases, whereas only twelve percent of the men were. But, even worse, at that same university the male professors outnumbered the female by a four-to-one margin. And that's a public school. She says Asquith is worse. Much worse."

Carrie rolled onto her side and cuddled closer to

Andrew's warmth. "Louise says that the few women who have been awarded tenure at Asquith are tokens. She says Asquith rewards women who don't make waves, who devote themselves solely to their teaching. She says she hasn't a chance to achieve tenure here." Carrie raised her head and rested it on her hand as she gazed down at her husband. "Is that true?"

Andrew raised his eyebrows, pursed his lips, and pillowed his head on his muscular arms. "Could be," he said, as if musing to himself. "There aren't all that many tenured female professors here, and come to think of it, the ones who *are* tenured are built like Sherman tanks—big, heavyset women who favor loose, baggy tweeds and severe hairdos."

Carrie frowned. "Oh, Andrew, why is it that a good-looking woman is so seldom taken seriously? There's this awful superstition that an attractive woman can't possibly have a brain, or be ambitious, or even be capable. We've been saddled with the horrible Victorian belief that only the dregs of womanhood care about their work, and then only because they must, because they're not attractive enough to get a husband who'll take care of them."

She sat up, hunching her knees under her chin and circling her legs with her arms as she propped her chin atop her knees. "I hate the injustice of it. The stupidity of it. Here we are, in late twentieth-century America, and we women are still victims of Victorian ignorance. Tremendous strides are being made in business and industry, yet Asquith University is still clinging to the nineteenth century." She suddenly glared at her husband. "And *you*'re a part of it!"

At that, Andrew sat up, laughing. "Hey, now, hold on just a darned minute, Carrie. Don't point that finger at me! I don't have anything to do with Asquith's informal rites concerning tenure for women."

"Ah, but you do, Andrew Everest! As a man, and as a member of Asquith's faculty, you participate in the repression of women at Asquith by merely standing by and letting it happen. Your passivity contributes to the general climate of repression."

Andrew stared at his wife as if seeing her for the first time. "My God, woman! You're calling me a male chauvinist conspirator!"

She nodded curtly. "Precisely."

He laughed in disbelief. "You've got to be kidding! Carrie, I've never done a thing to hold a woman back at Asquith—or anywhere else, for that matter. Do you think I'd have fallen in love with *you* if I liked my women passive and unassertive?"

"Love has nothing to do with it," she said staunchly.

"It sure as hell does!" he thundered, rising from the couch and parading in all his naked male glory to the fireplace, where he threw on another log and used the poker to stir the waning fire. He turned, put his hands on his lean hips, and stared stonily at his wife who sat saucily on the velvet sofa, the afghan having slipped to her waist, revealing the delightful mounds of her breasts. "Carrie Everest," he said warningly, "I'm beginning to think you're a revolutionary."

She threw up her hands. "Well, of course I am!" she said. "You've known that from the moment you met me. It's only now, when it hits too close to home, that it bothers you."

"That is not true," he countered angrily, his gray eyes flashing like gunpowder being touched with a match. He strode over to the couch, yanked off the afghan, and gathered his wife in his arms.

"What are you doing?" she shrieked, unwillingly throwing her arms around his neck to keep from falling as he carried her forcefully across the room toward the door.

"I'm taking you upstairs to bed."

When her shouted protests went unheeded, she resorted to getting him by his Achilles' heel: his sense of propriety. "Our clothes are still downstairs," she reminded him primly. "Whatever will Alma say when she sees them tomorrow?"

"Who the hell cares?" he muttered, shouldering open the door to their bedroom and advancing on the queen size bed. He stood still for a moment, holding her against his naked chest. Then he held out his arms and dropped her onto the satin coverlet, where she landed in a tumbled undignified heap. It took her a moment to find her balance; then she rolled onto her knees and placed her hands on her hips. "You manhandle me like that again, Andrew Everest, and it'll be the last time you touch me," she threatened, her green eyes flashing.

"You talk big, lady."

"I talk straight, buddy."

They stared at each other, eyes warring. Then Andrew's lips began to twitch with humor, sending Carrie's temper soaring. "Don't you laugh at me!" she roared, scrambling from the bed to stand before him, her forefinger poking ineffectually at the wall of his chest. "Do you hear me? I will not have you laugh at me!" She stared up into his gray eyes, hers still afire with rage.

Andrew let out a breath slowly and drew her into his arms, stroking her soft, silken back, his chin resting amid her curls. "Ah, Carrie," he murmured soothingly, "I do love you. You of the green, snapping eyes and flaring temper. You of the revolutionary zeal and hatred of injustice." He rocked her back and forth in his embrace. "You teach me so much."

Startled, Carrie pushed back from his embrace and studied his face. "I teach you?" she asked softly.

He delicately traced with his fingertip the lines of her face, down her cheek to the corner of her lips, finally letting his hand settle around the curve of her neck, his fingers gently massaging her nape. "Yes," he said, "you teach me. Oh, I've all manner of book learning, Carrie. I've grown up in this rarefied atmosphere of Asquith, with its traditions of intellectual searching and questioning, but I've never before come into such close contact with a mind so unfettered by musty conventions. You break all molds, Carrie. You look the old ways of doing things in the face and ask why. You're like fresh air in a closed-up old house. You clear out the cobwebs."

He sighed and let her go before sitting down wearily on the edge of the bed. "All along I thought I was learning to think for myself, but what I've really been doing is wearing a rut into my brain—a rut of forging steady habits, of accepting received opinion, of maintaining the status quo, of never rocking the boat." He sighed again. "Carrie, I'm beginning to wonder if we're going to have an easy time of it in this marriage of ours."

Concerned, Carrie sat down and put an arm across her husband's wide shoulders. "What are you saying? That we're not suited for each other?"

He turned his gaze on her and looked at her thoughtfully. "I know I love you more than I ever dreamed it was possible to love someone, but I also know that we're as different as two species of animal. You sweep into my life and expect me to think like you do, but I can't, Carrie. I'm me—stuffy, pompous Professor Everest."

She laughed out loud. "Hogwash! Was that man downstairs on the couch stuffy and pompous?" She rubbed her cheek affectionately against his muscular arm. "Oh, darling, of course we're different. That's probably why we love each other so much. You know, opposites attract, and all that stuff."

He nodded. "Yes, but, Carrie, what happens after the first glow wears off? We're going to clash. It's inevitable."

She shook her head at him, her eyes teasing. "You defeatist! You coward! You're creating a problem merely by suggesting there'll be one." She took his hands in hers and squeezed them tightly. "Andrew," she said softly, urgently, "we love each other. That's all that matters. Love truly *does* conquer all, you know."

He looked into her hope-filled eyes and felt a shaft of sadness shoot through him. One of the reasons he loved her was for her optimism, her boundless pleasure in the world, her refusal to be daunted by obstacles. She took the world by the throat and shook it until it gave in to her way of thinking. But he, more experienced, more moderate, knew the world didn't always give in so easily. One day his Carrie, his bright-eyed, wonderful wife, would come up against something that refused to change—and it just might be Asquith.

He felt a dart of fear in his midsection. And then what would happen to them? Would all that love she professed for him remain? Would the love they shared make it through the storm that might break over their lives? He sighed heavily, got up, and stripped back the coverlet.

"Go to bed," he said softly. "I'll be back in a minute."

She stared as he walked slowly across the thick wall-to-wall carpeting toward the door. "But where are you going?"

"Downstairs to get our clothes." He turned at the door and smiled a slightly embarrassed smile. "We wouldn't want Alma to find them."

Carrie began to laugh. "But you just said it didn't matter if Alma saw them."

He waved away her words. "That was in anger." He smiled again and disappeared from the doorway. Carrie lay back in bed and stared at the empty door.

They really were different, she realized. He really cared if Alma discovered evidence of their spontaneous lovemaking. It didn't matter a tinker's damn to her.

Settling back against the pillows, she suddenly remembered her game that morning in the dining room: "One for me, Grandfather. None for you." Maybe, just maybe, the old patriarch of the Everest family had scored more points than she had ever realized—scored them before she had even entered the game.

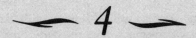

4

ANDREW WAS IMMERSED in the morning paper, but it didn't faze Carrie, for they were comfortably installed in the cheerful breakfast porch and his body was deliciously close. Close enough for her to smell the scent of his after shave. Close enough for her to reach out and caress his arm, neatly encased in a freshly starched white shirt. Close enough for her to slide her bare foot up and down his leg.

But she did none of these things. Andrew had more than satisfied her physical yearnings forty-five minutes ago in their four-poster canopied bed, which sang in its own special rhythm when they set it humming with their lovemaking. So she was content to sip her coffee and nibble her croissant, which crumbled into golden litter on her plate. She was content to gaze happily around the cozy room, approving of its sparkling windows curtained in a crisp blue and white check, its white wicker chairs cushioned in a tiny red, white, and blue print, its geraniums lining the windowsills.

Feeling as if nothing on earth could equal the heavenly peace she felt at the moment, Carrie looked absently toward Andrew. With her chin resting on her fist, she stared at the newspaper held so rigidly in front of his face. Rigidly. Why was he holding the paper so rigidly? Why were his knuckles turning white from the pressure?

"Oh, dear Lord," he groaned, lowering the paper slightly and peering over its top toward his wife. "Oh, Carrie, now you've gone and done it."

She frowned. "Done what?" she asked, sitting up straight.

He tapped the paper. "This. The letter you wrote to the editor."

Excitement burst over her. "It's in? My letter made it?" she squealed, jumping up from her chair to look over Andrew's shoulder. "Where? Show me."

He indicated the column, and Carrie read it out loud, her voice rising with excitement. "At a public university here in Connecticut," she read, "a study recently completed by the American Association of University Professors indicates alarming differences in the merit raises awarded male and female professors. Even more alarming to women is the fact that male professors outnumber females four-to-one. As a resident of Asquith and a member of the university community, I am concerned for women at our own esteemed university. We who should be in the forefront of movements for human rights seem to be dragging our feet. I am told that there are few opportunities for female professors here, and fewer still for those women to obtain tenure. It has come to my attention that, last year, only two women out of the twenty eligible were awarded tenure. We at Asquith, then, are eighteen talented women poorer. It is to be hoped that this year's tenure-granting will be far more equitable—and rewarding—for Asquith's able and talented female faculty members."

Satisfied with her efforts, Carrie leaned down impulsively and gave Andrew a resounding kiss on the cheek. Hugging him around the neck, she laughed delightedly. "What do you think?" she asked, excitement bubbling in her voice. "Think it'll get their attention?"

Andrew neatly folded the paper and placed it next to his napkin. Carrie followed his precise motions with dawning understanding. She backed away from him, circled precariously, and sat down quietly in her own chair, propping her elbows on the table and cupping her chin in her hands as she studied her husband's face.

"You didn't like it, did you?" she asked.

"Well, I can't say I didn't like it. It's a very good letter, as such letters go."

She felt her lips tremble with laughter. Now there was a pompous, stiff-upper-lip answer if she had ever heard one. "Hey, there," she said softly, reaching out with a finger to stroke the back of his strong hand. "It's me, remember? Your wife? Carrie? The one you can talk straight with?"

His gaze fell to the finger touching his hand. He then raised his eyes and met her gaze with clear unhappiness. How could he tell her how hurt he was? Men weren't supposed to be hurt. At least, they weren't supposed to show it. Men were the strong, stalwart ones, the ones with feelings bricked up behind six-foot walls. But, dammit, he *was* hurt. Hurt that Carrie had gone and written this letter—an inflammatory one at that—and never even discussed it with him. Couldn't she have snuggled up to him in bed one night and asked his opinion? Couldn't she at least have told him she'd already written a letter, already sent it in to the paper?

But how could he let her see his vulnerability? He'd have to sidestep that emotional part of it until he'd had time to think it over. For now, however, he could approach the issue from a more logical angle—that of his career . . . and the meaning of marriage.

"Look, Carrie," he said, reaching out to take her hand, "no one in Asquith attacks the university. The university is the town's chief employer, the chief source of economic power. As a shopkeeper you should realize that. You don't bite the hand that feeds you. Attacking Asquith . . ." He trailed off, feeling troubled. Carrie wasn't listening. Her green eyes were glaring, and he knew a storm was brewing.

Carrie narrowed her eyes and faked a dazzling, sarcastic smile. "Are we or are we not in a democracy? Or have we suddenly traveled back in time to sixteenth-century England, to an autocracy?"

Andrew snorted. Now she was trampling on *his* territory. But if she wanted a history lesson, he'd give her one.

"England in the sixteenth century was hardly an autocracy. The Magna Carta was signed in June of 1215 at Runnymede—"

"The hell with Runnymede!" Carrie shouted, standing up and planting her palms firmly on the tabletop. "Are you going to sit there and lecture me on history when my letter is the issue here?"

"Carrie, calm down."

"I will not calm down! I refuse to calm down!" At that the swinging door opened and Alma appeared in the doorway, her eyes round, her face ashen. Carrie waved her away. "It's okay, Alma. Andrew and I are just having a little domestic dispute."

Alma nodded uncertainly, darted a quick glance at Andrew, who nodded reassuringly, and promptly backed away and disappeared behind the swinging door.

Carrie took another breath and made an effort to lower her voice. "We were discussing my letter to the editor and my right as a citizen to write it. What really infuriates me, Andrew, is the way you're refusing to answer me!" Her voice had begun to rise again, and the heat of her temper was making her cheeks flame.

Andrew closed his eyes and prayed for patience. "It's not that you don't have a right, Carrie—"

"Then what is it?" she challenged, her five-foot-five-inch frame trembling.

Andrew picked up the paper and slammed it back down on the table, standing up to lean forward, nose to nose with his wife. "It's that you didn't think of me or my position and what such a letter might mean to me," he said, gray eyes flashing with as much fire as his wife's green ones. His hands were steepled on the tabletop, and he leaned forward even farther. "I just happen to be on the faculty of said university, my dear, and it seems not to have occurred to you that your letter, written in high dudgeon, might just have an adverse effect on my career."

She faltered, her gaze sliding away from his. "I don't see," she said in a low voice that had begun to shake slightly, "what my letter to the editor could possibly have to do with your career."

Andrew nodded. "That's just it, Carrie: You don't see. You think you're still single and carefree, and that any cause that comes your way is grist for the mill." He paused, breathing hard in an effort to keep his temper leashed. "What apparently isn't clear to you is that the wife of an Asquith professor has certain duties, responsibilities—"

"Oh!" Carrie's eyes widened and she looked up, crossing her arms in front of her, her back now ramrod straight. "Rubbish! Utter rubbish. Suddenly we're back in the sixteenth century, and the little wife is in reality the little serf!"

Andrew ran his hand back through his hair, letting out an exasperated sigh. "There's no reasoning with you."

She bristled at that. "Andrew Edward Everest, am I or am I not a separate being from you?"

"Oh, honey—"

"Just answer me," she commanded, shaking with anger.

He nodded wearily. "You're a separate person, Caroline."

"And do I or do I not have the right to my own convictions?"

He nodded again. "You do."

"Then," she said, slowly drawing herself up to her full height, "do I or do I not have the right to write any letter to any editor on any subject, even if I *am* married to you?"

"You do."

She nodded curtly, folding her arms again. "Case rests."

Andrew looked at her for a long moment, then said, "And do *I* or do I not have the right to a certain amount of loyalty from my own wife?"

"Loyalty?" she shrieked. "This hasn't anything to do with loyalty!"

"From your angle, it doesn't," he agreed, "but from

mine it does." He reached behind him, picked up his jacket from the back of his chair, and shrugged into it. "And it might just be advisable for you to ponder that, Carrie. You're no longer single. You're part of a pair now. And that means not always thinking of your own feelings but of looking at things from my viewpoint, also. You don't have just yourself to consider anymore, you see."

He turned on his heel and began striding toward the door, but Carrie stopped him. "And what about you, Andrew?" she yelled. "That was a lovely little speech, all calculated to elevate my guilt level, but it applies equally to you."

They stood staring at each other, each convinced of being right. Andrew's jaw worked angrily; then he turned and left.

Alone now, Carrie let her shoulders slump, and she drooped into her chair. There was more to this marriage business than first met the eye, she thought miserably.

"Interesting letter from your wife in the paper this morning, Everest," Nathan Ridley said as he poked his head around the office door. "She got the wind up a bit, wouldn't you say?"

Andrew glowered at his colleague. "Stuff it, Nathan," he said, and he swiveled in his chair to look out the window behind his desk. It was ten below zero outside, and as usual the window was coated with frost. Beneath it the ancient radiator hissed and knocked.

"Ah-ha!" Nathan Ridley said, entering the office and slamming the door shut. "Do I detect marital discord on the horizon?"

"You do not," Andrew replied coldly, turning back to glare at the man who had been his college roommate and who now shared his office. Nathan, too, was up for tenure, and it was generally thought he would get it. He was brilliant, his papers were published in the finest professional journals, his lectures were stimulating, and his research was impeccable. He was also still single, a self-avowed bachelor, happy to sample the wares of "all womanhood" as he put it and not get caught in the matrimonial trap.

Nathan unwrapped a long scarf from his neck, unbuttoned his coat and flung it carelessly across a chair, then rubbed his cold hands together vigorously, striding across the cramped office toward the coffee pot, which gurgled gently on a hot plate.

He laughed with pure pleasure as he poured himself a mug of coffee.

"I knew it," he said. "I do detect discord. Andy, old boy, you haven't been grumpy like this since before you got married. You had your first fight this morning, didn't you? And it was over the letter to the editor, wasn't it?"

Andrew scowled at his best friend, who grinned as he sat down and promptly put his feet up on Andrew's desk and began sipping his coffee. "You should really mark your calendar, Andy. This is a red-letter day—first fight and all that." He laughed at the blaze of anger in Andrew's gray eyes and leaned forward. "Do you know they're taking bets on how long you two will last?"

At that, Andrew stormed out of his chair. "I said stuff it, Nathan." He shoved the chair back and heard it thump against the radiator. He wandered the office, running his hand through his hair. Then he turned abruptly. "And I'll wager that *you*'re the one taking the bets, Nathan," he snapped.

Nathan grinned and held up a placating hand. "Not on your life. Since you've been married you've become infinitely easier to live with in this cramped little hole. I only bring you the news of the hour: Everyone's buzzing about Carrie's letter." His grin widened. "And you *did* fight with her about it, didn't you?"

Andrew slumped into his chair again, leaning forward to rest his head in his hands, his elbows propped on the cluttered surface of his desk. "Yeah. We fought." He stared down at an essay exam he was supposed to be correcting and absently noted a misspelled word. Nothing angered him more than seeing misspellings on papers. These kids at Asquith were supposedly the cream of the crop, and still they couldn't spell.

"Want to tell Uncle Nathan about it?"

"What?" His head came up, and for a moment he had to strain to remember what they'd been talking about. Then it came back to him, and he felt his heart dip. No wonder he'd tried to suppress it. He hated the thought of fighting with Carrie. And who had been right, anyway? He or she? Dammit all, why were things so complicated?

Nathan shook his head and leaned forward to put his own mug down on the overcrowded desktop. "It must have been a bad one—the fight, that is."

Andrew nodded. "And that damnedest part is, I don't know who was right—or if either of us was. I can see her point . . . but, dammit, I also can see mine."

Nathan held up a warning finger, a pose he often struck while lecturing. "Compromise, my dear boy, compromise. The stuff and stock of a good marriage."

"Who said that?"

"I did." Nathan grinned. "Aw, come on, cheer up. This will all die down in a day or two."

"Is it bad? The talk?"

Nathan shrugged. "Hopewell's red-faced with rage. Old Birdy—Oliver Birdwell—is stuttering and waving around the newspaper as if it contained a slur on his own character." He waved a dismissing hand. "Nothing you can't handle."

Andrew nodded, leaning forward to let his forearms rest on his thighs, his hands clasped loosely between his knees as he stared down at the floor. "But should I have to—that's the point. If Carrie had only thought before she sent that thing off to the paper."

"Ah-ha, I'm beginning to see the drift of your fight. She lifted that determined chin of hers and talked about principles or some such rot, and you called to mind her duties as the wife of a professor at Asquith."

Andy nodded glumly. "You're pretty much on target."

Nathan grinned wolfishly. "Never would have happened if you'd married Constance."

At that, Andrew's head came up like the crack of a whip. "Stuff it, Nathan," he repeated, grinning. "That's the one thing you could have said that makes me glad Carrie wrote the letter."

"Why do you think I said it?" Nathan asked gently.

Andrew studied his friend with speculative eyes. "Do you mean to say you actually approve of Carrie and me?"

Nathan grinned again. "You know my attitude toward marriage—like the plague, is how I view it— but yes, I do approve of you and Carrie. Seeing you two together is a little like being a child and believing in Santa Claus again." He removed his feet from Andrew's desk and stood up, stretching painfully. "Pulled a muscle playing racquetball," he grumbled, rubbing his shoulder and upper arm. "And the little coed I played with was rather athletic afterward. That didn't help matters any."

Andrew laughed. "Still chasing the coeds, eh?" He shook his head ruefully. "You're getting too old for that stuff, Nathan. It's time you found yourself a nice woman—the kind who'd rub liniment into your poor, ancient muscles after a hard game at the club—and settled down."

Nathan made an obscene gesture and, grinning, picked up a pile of books and strode out the door.

Andrew leaned back in his seat, propped his hands behind his head, and chuckled. Sometimes he thought that Nathan Ridley was the one reason he'd retained his sanity all these years at Asquith. Until he'd met Carrie, Andrew had had only Nathan to talk with. Only Nathan had shared his conflicting feelings for the university—they alternately loved and loathed it, yet neither had ever questioned his place in its system. Not until Carrie came along, Andrew thought, swiveling his chair to look out the ice-encrusted window. Leaning forward, he used his thumbnail to scrape a peephole in the frost and peered out. Below, students hurried to and from classes. Andrew's gaze drifted toward the fringe of trees along the border of the campus. Over there, a couple miles away, Carrie was tending to her bookshop. Once again the feeling overcame him, gripping him like a vise—he wanted to be with Carrie. Dammit, he wanted to be with Carrie...

"That will be seventeen fifty-nine, with tax," Carrie

said to her customer, looking up and smiling at the woman who was studying her with obvious interest. When their eyes met, the woman looked down and fumbled in her pocketbook for her wallet. "Uh . . . yes . . ." she said, sounding somewhat out of breath. "Seventeen fifty-nine." Then she looked stricken. "Oh, how foolish of me," she said, putting her hands to her cheeks and raising wide blue eyes to Carrie. "I forgot—I've only got a five with me."

Carrie smiled generously. "I can either hold the book for you, or you can put it on a credit card."

The woman looked away quickly, bit at her lip, and seemed to debate inwardly about something. "I'd planned to pay cash," she volunteered, "but . . ." Then she nodded decisively and took out a MasterCard. "Here," she said, blushing.

Carrie smiled reassuringly and fit the card into the credit card machine. As she reached for the proper receipt her gaze fell on the name embossed on the card. CONSTANCE HOPEWELL stared up at her in capital letters. Carrie felt her heart skip a beat and felt color rush into her own cheeks. "Oh, Miss . . . Miss Hopewell . . ." She looked up and forced a smile. "I've heard Andrew speak of you often." She held her hand out, Constance Hopewell took it hesitantly and shook it. Their eyes met for a second, then skittered away. Carrie busied herself with the charge information, produced the slip to be signed, and gave Constance Hopewell her receipt.

"You caught me," Constance said, her cheeks still pink. "I . . . I came to see you, really, not to buy a book."

Disarmed at her candor, Carrie smiled warmly. "Am I as bad as they all say?" she asked.

A small smile quivered on Constance's lips. She looked down with demure blue eyes. Although Constance seemed frightfully shy and insecure, Carrie thought her incredibly lovely, with no makeup to enhance her naturally beautiful features. She had that frail kind of English beauty: pale, flawless skin, blond hair, and cheeks that blushed without blusher.

"I . . . I think you're quite lovely," Constance said softly. "Not a bit like me."

Carrie felt a rush of compassion. "Strange that you should say I'm lovely," she said gently. "I was just thinking that about you."

Constance looked up, startled. "Me?" She shook her head in confusion and laughed nervously. "Now I know why Andrew married you: You're very kind." Then she blushed furiously. "Oh! But of course he married you because he loves you, too!" she stammered, looking as if she wanted the floor to open and swallow her up.

Carrie smiled. "I know what you meant. And I hope you'll . . ." She hesitated. She had been about to invite Constance to visit Andrew and her, but that might prove a bit awkward. "I hope you'll come in again. I encourage browsing, you know, and there's always a cup of hot coffee or tea or whatever."

Constance clutched her book to her breast and backed away toward the door, nodding. "Of course. I will. I really will." Her gaze left Carrie for a moment and wandered the comfortable store. "It's really lovely here. Not like a store at all. More like a home." She stopped at the door and looked at Carrie again. "And I think that's another reason Andy married you," she said softly, smiling slightly. "I think you must be the kind of woman who can make any house seem like a home." She blushed again, then turned and opened the door, admitting a rush of wind that grabbed at the wool scarf around her neck. Then the door closed, and Carrie looked out at the slight figure who battled the winds on the sidewalk.

How extraordinarily nice Constance was! Carrie thought. Whatever on earth had Andrew been thinking of all these years, not to marry her? Then she caught herself. What a ninny! If he'd married Constance, he couldn't have married Carrie!

She turned back to the cash register and rang up the sale, then thoughtfully began straightening the counter. There were three or four other customers in the store, idly perusing the shelves. Carrie smiled. They were probably all in the store to get warm, waiting for a bus perhaps. But if one wanted to buy something, her assistant, Sally, was always there, cheerful and helpful. Carrie could return to her small office and continue her ordering.

"Sally? Would you watch the store for me?"

Her young assistant looked up from unpacking books and nodded. "No problem, Carrie."

Carrie went into her office and shut the door. It wasn't often that she resorted to closing the door, but today she needed privacy, a chance to think without interruptions. As she took a seat at her cluttered desk her thoughts crept back to Constance.

What had Alma said? Something about everyone at Asquith expecting Andrew to marry her someday? Carrie stared out the window, only vaguely noticing the pedestrians who hurried by, their hands clutching their collars to their throats, the wind catching their hats and tumbling them along the sidewalk in a merry chase. Her thoughts were on that morning's scene in the breakfast room. Constance never would have written that letter to the editor...

Confused, Carrie stared sightlessly down at the desktop. Was Andy right? Had it been thoughtless of her to write the letter to the editor? But she believed in the cause, dammit!

Sighing, she shook away her thoughts and dragged her copy of *Publishers Weekly* toward her. She wouldn't think about it now. She'd just concentrate on her work.

5

CARRIE WAS BACK behind the counter when Louise Henderson swooped into the store a few hours later, her cheeks flaming with wind-whipped color, her heavy Tyrolean cape sweeping around her lithe figure like pontifical robes. She waved the Asquith *Express* in her hand, grinning from ear to ear.

"You've done it!" Louise exclaimed, rushing forward to hug Carrie robustly. "You've stirred up a hornet's nest with your letter to the editor. The English department is draping itself in sackcloth and ashes. Funeral dirges are more cheerful than my male colleagues. And I hear that Larry Hopewell and Ollie Birdwell are spitting mad."

At the mention of Andrew's associates in the history department, Carrie felt as if a huge hand had gripped her stomach, twisting it until it hurt. Oh, Lord. Andrew had been right. She'd gone about her business willy-nilly, never giving his position at Asquith a thought. Now he might be taking a lot of flak.

She looked away from Louise's shining eyes uneasily. "I can understand your knowing about the reaction in the English department, but how come you know what's going on in the history department?"

Louise unbuttoned her loden green cape and flipped it off the shoulders, letting it land gracefully on the counter. "There are two women in the history department," Louise explained, "and I've gotten to know them rather well in the past few months. They're both coming up for tenure, too, and of course we're all worried about it. There are a few other women as well—one in anthropology, two in math, and one in business."

Louise paused. "Carrie, I want to bring them with me to our Wednesday meeting this week. We're only a small group of seven women, and we need support." Louise pointed toward the newspaper that lay on the counter. "Whether you know it or not, by writing that letter, you've just given us exactly what we need—a voice in the community."

Carrie signaled to Sally to take over, led Louise into her office, and shut the door. "What do you expect to accomplish by bringing your friends here to our Wednesday group?" Carrie asked.

"More support. Pressure from the community. Asquith has taken the tack of keeping its dirty linen hidden. It keeps a low profile, hoping no one will question what's going on. What we want to do is bring the tenure question out in the open. And we need other women's support. Our Women's Wednesday group seems a logical place to start."

Carrie nodded and eased into her chair, indicating to Louise to take another. "I see."

Louise pulled up a chair, sat down, and leaned forward eagerly. "Carrie, what we want is a chance to talk to other women outside the university. Women are all sisters, Carrie. All we women are in this thing together." She eyed Carrie searchingly, then hopped up and hoisted herself onto a corner of Carrie's desk, her legs dangling as she went on enthusiastically. "Remember last month when Susie Cummings talked about how hard it was to go out and start making a living after her husband left her? You know it and I know it—it's because a woman makes fifty-nine cents to every dollar a man makes. Her husband will end up making a settlement out of their combined assets, and nothing will touch his salary. He'll be free and earning exactly what he's earned all along. Susie's new to the job market, without skills, barely able to make a living at entry-level wages."

Louise paused, then went on. "It's the same for women at Asquith, Carrie. We don't make the same salary the men do, even though some of us are better scholars, better lecturers, better researchers. The old-boy network still flourishes at Asquith, and until somebody challenges it, we're stuck with it. Only two women came up for tenure last year, Carrie, and both were denied it. Yet, those tenured slots were later filled by men." Louise shook her head. "To use a time-honored cliché, something's rotten in the state of Denmark."

Carrie felt torn. She believed in everything Louise was saying, but her fight with Andrew that morning still reverberated in her head. Then she decided that, if he understood the issue more clearly, surely he would want her to stand up for what she believed in. Besides, she wasn't taking the lead in any kind of organized protest; she was merely inviting certain female faculty members at Asquith to come to a group meeting on Wednesday. That was how they had begun: Any woman with a concern she wanted to share with other women was welcome in the Women's Wednesday group. To deny this right to female faculty members at Asquith simply because Carrie was afraid Andrew would be offended was ridiculous.

"Well, I can't see any harm in having your friends come and talk at the meeting Wednesday night," Carrie said, smiling. "The whole point of our group is that we're open to any woman who's interested."

Louise slid off Carrie's desk and clapped her hands joyously. "I knew you'd be for it. Any woman who wrote a letter like the one you wrote would have to be."

At the mention of the letter Carrie felt another stab of doubt. She tried to ignore it, laughing as she combed her fingers through her unmanageable mane. "Well, it didn't make a hit in *my* house, let me tell you that!"

Louise settled slowly into a chair. "I see. Care to talk about it?"

Carrie looked down at her hands. "Andrew seemed to feel I'd somehow been disloyal to him in writing that letter."

Louise sat back, her face serious. "I hadn't thought about that—his being on the faculty of Asquith. That must make it difficult for you."

Carrie began examining her nails. "The only thing that's difficult is getting used to being married. Andrew went on and on about my starting to think like a wife instead of acting as if I were still single."

Louise nodded. "Hmm. Jack, my husband—" She smiled. "I don't mention Jack often in the group, do I? Well, anyway, Jack and I have had these . . . what would you call them? Conflicts? He's terribly supportive in so many ways, but occasionally he rears up and acts like an enraged bear when I get particularly hot under the collar about certain issues."

"How's he acting about the tenure issue?"

"He's all for me and my cause. He's a professor at Yale and thinks Asquith is woefully behind the times—though from what he says, I'm not sure Yale is much better about awarding tenure to its female faculty."

"Well, how do you negotiate the 'hot spots' in a marriage?" Carrie asked. "It's a bit like culture shock: One day you're single and your own woman, and the next you're married and your husband's complaining that you're not asking his advice."

Louise laughed, slid down low in her chair, and crossed one booted leg over the other. "It's ridiculous, isn't it? Jack and I always fight about the dumbest things, like who does the laundry or picks up his dirty socks." She sat up straighter, her eyes suddenly blazing. "I mean, I just get livid when Jack leaves his socks on the bedroom or bathroom floor. And when I confront him about it, he laughs it off, makes a joke out of it. But if I should ever forget to put an olive in his martini, I'm dead. He roars around the place for an hour, telling me how inconsiderate I am."

Carrie began to chuckle. "It's totally ridiculous. Whoever invented marriage in the first place?"

Louise rolled her eyes. "Men, of course. Otherwise they'd have to stay at home and let their mothers take care of them."

Carrie stopped laughing and looked at Louise with deep interest. "But you're happy, aren't you? I mean, if you had to do it over again, you would, wouldn't you?"

"In a minute," Louise said, smiling. "He may leave his socks around the house, but at least he's there to leave them. I can't bear the thought of a life alone, of one toothbrush in the bathroom, one towel, one washcloth..."

Carrie's eyes misted, and she pretended to look in her desk for a pen. "Well!" she said brightly, standing up and opening the door to her office. "We'll see you and the others Wednesday, then."

Louise stood up and hugged Carrie, then walked out and searched for her cape. Fastening it around herself, she looked up and smiled. "Thanks, Carrie— for the letter and for being you."

Carrie shook her head. "Go on home, Louise. Jack's socks are probably waiting for you."

Grinning, Louise turned and hurried from the store, leaving Carrie looking wistfully after her. If only she had mundane things like dirty socks to fight about with Andrew. In their case it was the big issues—like loyalty and wifely duties—that were causing problems.

Andrew strode through the snow, his hands thrust deep into his overcoat pockets as he struggled against the headwind on his way home. His mouth was set in a grim line. He didn't know what made him angrier—Larry Hopewell's loudmouthed annoyance at Carrie's letter, or the determined thrust of Carrie's chin when she had confronted him at breakfast.

It had been their first real fight. He had walked out on her, not bothering to say a civil word, and for the first time since they'd dated, he hadn't kissed her good-bye. How should he act when he saw her? Ignore the whole thing and hope that it went away? Continue his hard line and not give in to her? Forgive her? Kiss her? Make a joke out of it?

Miserable, he kicked at a pile of snow, then winced

with pain and cursed when he realized that the snow was frozen solid and he had come perilously close to breaking his toe. Dammit, Carrie wasn't the kind to let this thing blow over. And why should he forgive her? Wasn't he partially right also? For the first time he thought he understood the glacial silences that had existed from time to time between his grandparents and, later, between his parents. Marriage was a damned difficult business.

He chuckled dryly over Nathan's words. *Compromise—the stuff and stock of a good marriage*. But what did Nathan know about marriage? He'd never been there—hadn't the slightest desire to do so. It was one thing for Nathan to sit in their warm office with his feet up and talk blithely about marriage and how to make it work. It was another thing entirely to *be* married, to *have* to make it work.

Sighing gustily, Andrew turned down his street and lifted his face to the wind. The street never failed to impress him. It was lined with elegant Federal-style brick residences, each professionally landscaped, with a line of maples arching over the street, their limbs now naked except for their covering of ice. Practically everyone on this street was somehow connected with Asquith University. Most had lived here as long as the Everests, and that meant generations. It was like stepping back in time. On this street only old-fashioned gas lanterns were allowed. There were no modern streetlights, no unsightly power lines to mar the perfection. It was all so genteel, so refined.

Andrew stopped in front of his home and looked at the warm glow of lamps shining in the windows, welcoming him home. He stared at the gracious brick facade, the wide, welcoming double doors surmounted by a fanlight, the broad, low brick steps leading up to the doors with their twin pineapple-shaped brass door knockers.

He could picture his grandmother as she had been so long ago, seated in the "drawing room" as she chose to call it, her long skirts trailing about her chair as she embroidered, her slim, aristocratic frame bent over the tiny stitches, her silver hair glowing in the soft lamplight.

And his mother—tall, lean, with the grace of a thoroughbred, her hair sprinkled with silver, her face unlined, her posture impeccable, as she sat on the brocaded formal sofa in the living room and poured tea from a Revere sterling tea service.

He sighed at his memories. Two women cut from the same cloth—refined, genteel, unquestioning of their place in life. And now there was Carrie.

With his hands in his pockets, he gazed absently at the study windows. He knew Carrie would be there, probably sitting in her favorite chair, her feet tucked underneath her as she read and sipped a drink. She said she liked to sit there because it made her feel closer to him when he wasn't there.

Carrie. So different from the other two Everest wives. Yet, he loved her with a passion he hadn't known he possessed. Then he remembered her obstinacy, her stubbornness, her wild streak of independence, and he felt his emotions heat up. What was the matter with him tonight? He felt ready to take on a bear.

Grimly he strode along the walk that led to the back door, letting himself in quietly, shrugging out of his coat, and depositing his briefcase on the small table in the hall. He pushed open the kitchen door and was greeted by the aroma of leg of lamb and carrots cooking. Alma turned and grinned at him.

"Miss Carrie's in the study, Mr. Andy."

Andrew stared at Alma in surprise. Miss Carrie? Since when had Alma taken to calling an Everest wife by her first name? He saw Carrie's hand in this little scenario, stirring up things in the Everest pot. He nodded curtly to Alma, let the door swing shut, and strode determinedly toward the study. When he opened the door, he found Carrie curled up in his chair, just as he expected, her eyes pensive as she stared into the fireplace, her chin resting on her fist. She only looked up when he shut the door with unnecessary force.

"Oh! You're home!" She sprang from the chair, her eyes glowing as she ran to greet him, throwing her arms around him and kissing him softly on the lips.

Rubbing her forehead back and forth against his square chin, she whispered, "It must be freezing outside. You feel like an icicle." She lifted her head. "How about some sherry or brandy? We've got to warm you up."

When he said nothing her green eyes narrowed, and she stepped back. "Ah," she said, nodding judiciously, "bad day at Black Rock?"

"Dammit, Carrie," he exploded, pointing toward the chair she'd just vacated. "That's my chair!"

Her eyebrows rose as she turned slowly to study the object of Andrew's wrath. Then she turned back. "So it is," she observed mildly. "You're particularly observant today, Professor Everest."

His jaw twitched in anger. "It isn't bad enough that you move in here and disturb all the Everest traditions, but you have to take my chair in the bargain!"

Carrie faced him calmly. "I never intended to take *your* chair, as you put it. But if my sitting in your chair makes you so uncomfortable, I'll simply buy another for myself. Does that suit Your Highness?"

Andrew stomped over to the console table and poured three fingers of bourbon into a squat, very rare piece of cut glass. He downed half of it in one swallow. He stood with his eyes squeezed shut, feeling the heat of the liquid burn its way into his gut, then turned toward Carrie and said, "That will be fine. Buy anything you want. Just leave me to my chair in peace."

Carrie drew herself up to her full height, snapped to attention, and saluted. "Yes, *sir!*" she shouted.

At the console table Andrew felt his nerves tingle. By God, the little demon was laughing at him! It wasn't bad enough that he'd taken abuse all day from Larry Hopewell and Ollie Birdwell as he defended her letter vociferously. Now she was making fun of him! He set his glass down hard, then winced as he thought of what he might have done: smashed the glass—and it was damned expensive—and perhaps left a dent in the precious mahogany his grandfather had imported from England.

From across the room Carrie observed his wincing and folded her arms. "What's the matter?" she taunted gently. "Afraid you've hurt an Everest antique?"

He glared at her. "Well, it's a damned good thing *one* of us cares about them!"

Carrie's amusement boiled into anger. "Okay," she said tightly, pointing to the chair. "What's all this about? A grown man just doesn't storm into a room and start babbling about a chair. There's more to it. Come on, Andrew, come clean."

"You know what it's about, Carrie. We left off this morning, and we're taking it up again now."

Carrie let out a deep breath. "So, it's still the letter."

"It's the letter and the chair and Alma calling you Miss Carrie and not eating in the dining room and my having to defend you against all my colleagues because you took it into your pretty little head to write a letter to the editor."

"Andrew, when I wrote that letter I never, ever, meant for it to hurt you in any way. Can't you understand that? The letter had nothing to do with you."

"But that's just it, Carrie—it does. I'm in the middle here, married to a woman who's decided to take on Asquith University single-handedly, yet working for the university at the same time. I feel stuck between Scylla and Charybdis."

"Which am I? The rock or the whirlpool?"

"Neither!" he snapped. "All I see right now is a little five-foot-five bit of a thing who's come into my family home and turned it upside down. And you're not satisfied with wreaking havoc here; you have to get into the act at Asquith, thereby endangering everything my family has built up over the last hundred years."

"The only thing your precious family has built up, Andrew Everest, is a tradition based on fear—fear of being themselves, of defying society and thinking for themselves, of not being 'in' and 'accepted' by the elite." Carrie marched forward and stood in front of her husband. "And fear of letting their tempers get out of control, because if they do, they might damage one of their precious *antiques!*"

Andrew stared at her, his facial muscles twitching with agitation; then he turned, picked up the expensive glass, and hurled it across the room at the fireplace. It struck the brick with such impact that it shattered into thousands of brilliant shards that reflected the radiance of the fire in the hearth.

Carrie stood dumbfounded, staring at the glitter of shattered glass. She slowly lifted her gaze to Andrew. He stared back at her, his gray eyes frozen in anger and defiance. They were still caught in a silent trance when Alma opened the door and cheerily announced that dinner was ready.

Carrie reacted first. She turned toward Alma and smiled weakly. "I'm not feeling very well, Alma. I think I'll go upstairs and lie down. Perhaps Andrew will want to have his dinner in the dining room."

Andrew heaved a deep breath and ran a hand over his face. "No, Alma, just put it away, please. I'm really not hungry either."

Silently Alma withdrew and closed the door. Carrie turned on her heel and hurried across the carpet, caught the doorknob, flung open the door, slammed it shut after her, and hurried up the stairs toward the bedroom.

In the study, Andrew stared at the broken glass that littered the area around the hearth. Finally he began to clean up the mess. When he had safely deposited the glass in a wastebasket, he switched off the lights and walked slowly up the graceful, curving staircase. What could he say to Carrie? His behavior was indefensible. Never in his life had he reacted so violently. He ran his hand through his hair and stopped on the top step and observed the crack of light that glowed under their closed bedroom door. He turned off the hall light and was immediately enveloped in darkness. Only the sliver of light from their bedroom remained.

How ironic, he thought. That light was so like Carrie. Not long ago he had remarked that he had spent his life in darkness until her. Then it had been as if the sun had come out for the first time. Slowly he advanced, then hesitated, his hand on the doorknob, wondering how she would receive him. He had no right to expect forgiveness. Somehow, though, he had to find a way to apologize. He would have to make her see that he loved her beyond everything, that there was nothing more important than she.

Taking a steadying breath, he turned the knob and pushed the door open. Carrie was standing at the window, holding the drapes back with one hand, gazing up at the sky. He must have made a noise, or perhaps she just sensed his presence, for she came out of her reverie, turned suddenly, and saw him. She dropped the drapes, and her eyes searched his.

He stepped forward. "Carrie—"

Before he could say another word, she was rushing across the room, throwing herself into his arms, hugging him fiercely, murmuring his name over and over. "Oh, Andrew," she whispered. "Oh, my darling Andrew."

He put his strong arms around her and lowered his face, inhaling the fresh, sweet scent of her hair, cradling her against him. He was vibrantly aware of her lithe body molded against his, of its warmth, its sweet beauty, its incredible softness.

"Carrie," he murmured, rocking her back and forth to comfort her. "There is nothing on this earth that matters more to me than you. Nothing." Then he held her just far enough away from him so that he could look into her misty eyes. He smiled lovingly, regarding her as if she were a most precious jewel. "Is that clear, Carrie? Nothing is as important to me as you. Not this house, nor the precious antiques, nor my job at Asquith. Nothing."

Carrie's eyes cleared of their tearful mist, and she looked up at him with infinite tenderness and love. Slowly she reached up and slid her hand through his hair, then pulled his head down and kissed him gently.

"Andrew," she whispered against his lips. "I love you so very much."

He groaned and pulled her closer into his embrace, burying his head in the curve where her shoulder met her neck. "Carrie, forgive me. I can't explain it. Something in me snapped. I'm changing, Carrie, and I don't know what's happening to me. Suddenly I'm doing things I've never done before, feeling things I've never felt."

"Is that the first time you've ever lost your temper?" she asked quietly.

He nodded. "Yes. And it's scary."

She smiled and hugged him. "I know. Feelings *are* scary, Andrew. Even the good ones. But I think we have to learn to trust our feelings, to talk about them with each other."

He leaned down and whisked her up from the floor and into his arms. Whooping, she flung her arms around his neck and started laughing.

"What are you doing?" she cried, all anger gone, replaced by passion.

"Taking you to bed," he said, his voice low and intimate. He carried her to the four-poster, lowered her onto it, settled down beside her, and began to unfasten the buttons of her blouse. Then he slid his hand inside her blouse and deftly unfastened the front catch of her bra. His hand cupped the small weight of her breast, and he lowered his lips and kissed her reverently.

"I love you, Caroline," he whispered, his breath warm against her lips. "I love you."

Smiling, eyes suddenly misty again, she put her arms around his neck and pulled his head down to hers. "Love is all there is," she whispered. "Love is all there is."

— 6 —

CARRIE FLIPPED THE calendar and sighed. It was the first of March. Where had February gone? She looked up and smiled at her husband, who had just finished his scrambled eggs and was about to begin scanning the stock market report, a ritual that had become an increasingly important part of his day.

Sighing, she looked at the stack of bills arrayed in front of her. No use putting it off any longer. While Andrew made the decisions about stocks that would assure his vast inheritance's continued growth, she would write the checks and pay the bills. Methodically she set about her task.

Fifteen minutes later she had a stack of envelopes in front of her, ready to be mailed. Satisfied that she had accomplished the tedious but necessary chore, she scanned the calendar for birthdays, anniversaries, and other important dates so she could buy cards if necessary. Her eyes lit on March 16, the date of the Edward Haynes Everest Memorial Lecture. It was an annual event in the history department, and this year the distinguished scholar John Ransom Wilders would speak.

Carrie pondered whether to have a small dinner

party or not. Since her letter to the editor had been published in the paper, she felt she was persona non grata among Andrew's colleagues. Giving a small, intimate dinner party might be just the way to make amends. She would invite the Hopewells and the Bird-wells.

Her mind veered off as she remembered Constance Hopewell, the shy, lovely young woman who had snuck into Book Ends to "spy" on Andrew Everest's new wife. Even then Carrie had liked Constance automatically and had wanted to invite her to dinner. Only the knowledge that Constance had supposedly loved Andrew for years had kept Carrie from issuing an invitation.

But now the opportunity presented itself. If Carrie was inviting Constance's parents, it seemed only logical to issue an invitation to their daughter. If Constance was uncomfortable with the idea of being a guest in the home of Andrew and his new wife, then she could always make an excuse and refuse the invitation.

But if Constance did accept the invitation, and if everyone else attended, there would be an uneven number. While Carrie didn't mind not having everyone paired off neatly, she thought Constance might feel uncomfortable being at the dinner unescorted—especially in the home of the man she had once presumably wanted to marry. It would be rather like rubbing salt into an open wound, and Carrie had no desire to do such a thing to Constance. Constance should be a friend, not an enemy. And it wouldn't hurt her to stop mooning over losing Andrew and begin to socialize and meet other men. Constance was much too lovely a woman to hide herself in the gloomy Hopewell house.

But whom to invite as an escort for Constance? Carrie nibbled at the end of her pen and stared out the window into the backyard, her thoughts riffling through the available men she knew. For some reason Nathan Ridley's name kept coming up. She would slap it back into place and try to think of someone else, but up would pop Nathan again like a persistent puppy.

Carrie smiled to herself. One could hardly call Mr. Ridley a puppy! With his wild, curly hair and lanky frame, he was more like a bloodhound.

Andrew's amused voice broke into Carrie's thoughts. "And what is making you smile like the Cheshire cat, Mrs. Everest?"

Startled, Carrie shook her head and laughed. "I was just thinking of someone and how he reminded me of a— Oh, never mind." She waved her hand and dismissed her thoughts about Nathan. Knitting her brow, she looked solemnly at Andrew. "What do you think of our having a small dinner party the night of Professor Wilders's lecture?"

Andrew shrugged. "Sounds fine." He grinned. "Does this mean the honeymoon is over? No more candlelit dinners for two? Are we 'receiving guests' now?"

Carrie grinned back. "I thought it was about time we had some guests, yes. We can't slink off into the bedroom after *every* dinner, or we may end up with *more* than a dozen kids."

Andy's gray eyes lazily surveyed Carrie's trim figure. "I see no signs of any imminent little Everests."

"True."

"Is this your gentle way of telling me you don't want a dozen kids?" he asked, grinning crookedly.

Carrie giggled. "No, it's my cockeyed way of saying I'd like to make amends with certain esteemed members of the history department. After writing that letter to the editor, it seems only wise to do something to get back in their good graces, not only for my sake, but for yours."

Andrew got up, pulled Carrie from her chair, and put his arms around her. "Have I told you lately you make a pretty darned good wife?" he whispered, letting his lips pay homage by seeking the vibrating pulse in her neck.

Carrie closed her eyes and melted into Andy's embrace. "Uh-uh," she murmured, half saying no and half moaning in ecstasy.

Andy held her close, inhaling her scent, feeling her warmth, once again wishing he didn't have an eight-o'clock class. Right now he could very easily tote his little bundle of passion back upstairs to the canopied bed and make a day of loving her. As it was, he was firmly committed to a lifetime of loving her. She was his, and he was hers, and he was satisfied for things to stay that way forever.

He released her reluctantly with a lingering kiss she wanted to prolong, but he used all his willpower to resist. Perhaps if he got her back on the subject of her dinner party he would sidetrack her and thus hold his own passion in check.

"Who exactly were you thinking of inviting to this party?" he asked, his voice low, his hands refusing to leave her lithe body, lingering on her upper arms in a gentle caress.

"Oh," she answered breathily, eyes still half closed with desire, "just the Hopewells and the Birdwells and . . ." Her answer drifted off as his lips descended

despite his best intentions. There was no use fighting
it, he thought hazily. When he was near Carrie he
was a sitting duck.

After a few moments he summoned all of his re-
solve and tried once more to relinquish her. "It's nearly
eight, Carrie. I'll miss my class."

She gazed up at him with liquid green eyes, eyes
that clearly sent the message that she adored him, that
she didn't care one whit if he missed his class or not.
He watched as she reluctantly pulled from his embrace
and nodded.

"All right," she said. "Go. Otherwise I'll take you
by the hand and lead you back upstairs, and heaven
knows when I'll let you out of my sight again!"

He grinned down at her. "That is the one thing you
could have said that just might convince me to skip
class this morning."

She lifted her chin and grinned back. "Why else
do you think I said it?"

Laughing, Andrew leaned over, kissed her quickly,
and rushed from the breakfast room, leaving Carrie
leaning back against the table, a bemused, satisfied
smile on her face.

Carrie sat at her desk in the bookstore, writing out
formal invitations on those absurdly tiny pieces of
formal stationery the saleswoman in the bridal department at G. Fox's in Hartford had sold her. Her
name, Mrs. Andrew Edward Everest Jr., was en-
graved in gold leaf on ivory vellum.

She felt vaguely as if she were playacting at being
a grownup. Always before, when she was single and
entertaining, she had merely picked up the phone and
called her friends to invite them for pizza and beer or

a huge pot of chili. Her most lavish parties had consisted of baked chicken and fresh vegetables—certainly not up to the aesthetic level she must attain for the upcoming dinner party.

She took special pains to write slowly and carefully to ensure that her usual harum-scarum chicken-scratch penmanship would be readable. Only at the end did she allow herself to sign her name in her usual flamboyant scrawl.

She licked the envelopes, sealed them, affixed stamps, and took a deep breath. Her first attempt at formal entertaining. She bet the other Everest women had never been as nervous as this. It had all probably come very naturally to them. No doubt they'd been weaned on pâté de foie gras, truffles, and sweetbreads, while Carrie's diet as an infant had been strained peas and carrots.

Staring out the window at the pedestrians hurrying by, Carrie wondered what happy quirk of fate had brought Andrew Everest into her store that day last September, what chemistry had made her stomach flip-flop at the same time his did. What mischievous god had gotten her married to one of the wealthiest men in New England?

The Everest wealth was old money, amassed when a dollar meant a dollar and built up now over a century by the judicious investments of Andrew's grandfather and father. Andrew seemed to have the same knack for making money make more money. He could read stock market printouts, pore over various firms' annual reports and financial statements, and almost by intuition buy the stocks for twenty-five cents that soared to twenty-five dollars six months later. His ability to pick winners was uncanny.

Carrie's background hadn't exactly prepared her for her new lifestyle. While all Andrew's money, his beautiful home, and his employment of a house-keeper-cook hadn't overwhelmed her, she still felt she was a plain old all-American girl at heart.

Her parents, both radical, leftist lawyers who worked out of a storefront law office in the slums of Hartford, hadn't placed much emphasis on money. Instead they had implanted in her a desire for absolute truth, for emotional honesty, for compassion toward the poor and downtrodden. Since childhood she'd been a sucker for every lame dog and homeless cat, for every bird with a broken wing. Always, always, she'd taken the side of the underdog.

It was in her genes, she supposed, just as Andrew's astuteness at money-making, his reverence for knowledge, and his sense of honor and tradition were in his. They were the products of their backgrounds: Andrew essentially conservative, Carrie essentially liberal. And while Andrew's parents had fostered in him a desire not to sanctify the past and not to rock the boat, her parents had nourished in her a sense of fair play and an urgency to speak out on issues rather than take a back seat. Her parents had also laughed a lot and had cultivated friendships with everyone from ballet managers to policemen. Carrie's childhood had been exciting and free-spirited. Andrew's, she thought, had probably been far from that.

She shuddered to think of what it had been like growing up in the rarefied atmosphere of that mansion in the shadows of the august Asquith University. She doubted that a youthful Andy had ever been allowed to laugh and run around the house with total abandon. She couldn't imagine his parents allowing him to straddle the fine mahogany banister of the elegant, curving staircase and slide down it, whooping like a fire engine. It wouldn't have been "proper." Carrie gazed down at the "proper" invitations to her dinner party. They were out of character for her, but she had married into Andrew Everest's world, and for his sake she sometimes had to try to make the best of it. To learn to compromise, as Andrew had implied she was unwilling to do. Constant rebelling would only end in hurting their chances for a successful marriage.

She smiled as she thought of their breakfast conversation. Perhaps children, lots of children, were the answer. That dignified old house would be enlivened by the shouts of children's laughter, by their tears, by their skinned knees, by their kites flying high above the graceful maples. Picnics, bicycles propped up against the garage, puppies and kittens romping across the manicured lawns. Carrie felt shivers go down her arms at the thought of bearing Andrew's children. Oh, yes, lots of children.

Her parents, she knew, would be thrilled. Although they had tried ceaselessly to have more children, she had been their only child. They would embrace grandchildren and instill in them a sense of wonder at the world, a need for compassion, a desire for justice and truth, and a willingness to fight for what one believed in.

Thinking about her parents, Carrie laughed as she remembered their reaction upon meeting Andrew, whom she had announced she was going to marry.

"But he's so...so..." Her mother had stared at Carrie when they were alone, apparently unable to understand what Carrie saw in Andrew Everest, a conservative product of everything she and Carrie's father had fought all their lives.

"Staid?" Carrie asked, supplying a word she thought her mother might be searching for.

Her mother nodded. "I thought you'd grow up and marry a forest ranger, or an artist, or maybe a Hell's Angel. But, Carrie, a professor? At Asquith?"

Carrie took her mother's hand, pulled her down onto the couch, and put her arm around her shoulders.

"Mother, it's like this," she said gently. "You fight for your causes in your way, and I fight for mine in another. Andrew is . . ." She searched the ceiling for the words to explain her attraction. Then she giggled. "Andrew's hell on wheels in the bedroom, Mother. That's one reason for marrying him. But there's another, more important reason. He's solid. He's stable. He's like a rock, Mother. And I need that stability in my life. You've encouraged me to be free-spirited, and on my own I'm given to impulsiveness. Andrew steadies me."

She paused, considering. "On the other hand, Andrew can tend to be buttoned up and wrapped so tightly in his world that he could suffocate unless someone lets some air in. Well, *I* let the air into his life. We complement each other; we fill each other's needs. But most important, Mother, I love him. He is a wonderful man, with a sense of justice and moral values he's too modest even to know he possesses. He's a very fine human being, and I love him. I don't think I'll ever stop loving him, Mother. Ever."

Her mother smiled and drew her close and kissed her lightly on the forehead before releasing her. "The only thing your father and I have ever wanted for you, Carrie, is that you live your own life. That's what it's all about. We've never wanted you to do something simply to please us. It's your life, darling, and it wouldn't matter to us if you ended up marrying a Tibetan yak driver, as long as you were doing what you wanted to do."

Carrie had smiled and hugged her mother. "I knew you'd understand."

Carrie's musings were interrupted when she heard Sally calling for assistance. Glancing out the office, she was surprised to see a line of customers at the desk and Sally frenetically trying to help them all at the same time. Carrie happily left her office and pitched in. For the rest of the day she was oblivious to anything but the constant ring of the cash register and the steady stream of customers.

Wednesday night came. At six o'clock Carrie closed Book Ends and got ready for the Wednesday-night group to meet. They started arriving at six-fifteen, coming in on a gust of wind, coats blown about, hair in snarls, all chattering and laughing, filled with zest and spirit.

She fussed about, taking coats, getting them hot chocolate, and settling them in front of the crackling fire at the back of the cheery store.

When everyone had arrived, Carrie looked at the group in amazement. All of the usual Wednesday-night group were here, and the seven faculty members from Asquith, too. From a small, informal group they had suddenly grown into almost a formal meeting. Looking around her, she felt the excitement that stirred the air.

Carrie cleared her throat, and the group fell silent, all faces turned to her. "Some of you were here when Louise Henderson spoke at our last meeting. She talked about a problem facing the female faculty members at Asquith. She came to me later and asked if she could invite six other faculty members, all of whom are coming up for tenure at Asquith." Carrie paused, looking around at the faces, seeing interest and anticipation in all of them. "Tenure, if you're not acquainted with it, is, to put it as simply as possible, job security for a professor."

She launched into a detailed explanation of all the ins and outs of the tenure system for those who were not yet acquainted with it. When she finished she nodded to Louise. "With that background I'll turn everything over to Louise Henderson, Assistant Professor of English at Asquith, and her six colleagues."

Louise smiled wryly. "Well, here we are—the Magnificent Seven."

There was a ripple of laughter and some squeakings of the ancient Windsor chairs as a few people changed positions, and the quiet fell once again.

"First of all, let me introduce you to my colleagues." When she had done so, she paused, lit a cigarette, puffed on it languidly with all the timing of a masterly actress, exhaled the smoke in a thin blue line, and spoke. "We're all coming up for tenure, and not one of us thinks we have a snowball's chance in the tropics. We came here tonight simply to tell you what we're up against. Our aim, of course, is to garner support within the community from other women. Since I've been a member of the Women's Wednesday group almost from its inception, I thought this might be a logical place to start. But now I'll let Irma give you a few statistics."

Irma Fahey, with flaming red hair and a face full of freckles, wore wire-rim glasses, a conservative suit of gray flannel, and a silk scarf knotted at her throat. As she spoke, her delicate hands gestured in the air. "According to recent statistics, women make up only 35.4 percent of the college and university faculty across the country. At Asquith the figures are depressingly lower; women make up about 4 percent of the faculty here. And on the average we make less than our male counterparts—about a hundred dollars a week less. Yet, we have the same degrees, the same educational requirements, and often better academic records.

"We're fighting the old absurd notion that women don't need to make as much money as men because women aren't the breadwinners." She snorted her derision. "In point of fact, many of us *are* the breadwinners. Many of us divorced with children, and our ex-husbands quite often neglect to pay their child support. True, some of us are married, but often we're working to help our husbands get another degree or take time off to—do research—or we're simply working to help make ends meet. We literally are the breadwinners in many instances, but that's not the point!"

She took a calming breath. "You've got to forgive me. I get so darned heated up when I think about it."

Everyone laughed and encouraged her to go on. She paused, then continued more calmly. "The point is, we shouldn't be paid lower wages just because we're women. We should get equal pay for equal work. And as for tenure—Oh, gracious, tenure."

She threw up her eloquent hands in despair. "Asquith is unbelievable. They seem to hire women as tokens, then they get rid of us by not granting us tenure. Outwardly the boys are saying: 'Look, see how liberal and modern we are? We hire women.'

Then they shake their grizzled gray heads mournfully and say: 'Too bad they just don't measure up. Look at these deplorable tenure statistics.'"

Irma smiled wryly. "I've been up against this before. When I was working to get my Ph.D., I had a full-time job in a firm that had been given the official word from Washington: Hire women. Well, they did hire women, but they made damn sure those women didn't stay. Four very talented, able women were forced out of that place because they couldn't take the heat their male employer put on them. Yet, he could hold his head up, holier than anyone, and say he was *trying* to hire women; the problem was that they were too emotional to perform adequately."

Irma shook her head. "It's so frustrating to be patronized by a bunch of old men who don't want us in their private club." She looked at Carrie. "That letter you wrote some weeks back was the first public acknowledgment that there's a real problem at Asquith. Everyone else has been sweeping it under the rug. We women on the faculty have been working our tails off the past few years, hoping things would have changed by the time we came up for tenure, but we were fooling ourselves." Irma heaved a sigh. "Things haven't changed, and they won't until we force them to."

"Okay," Carrie said, "so what can we do?"

Louise spoke up. "Simply listening is good enough, if that's all you feel you can do at this time. We need support from other women, both in the university and outside it. I guess we're here to ask that at least a couple of you do what Carrie did—write a letter to the editor. Stir things up a bit."

Carrie laughed self-mockingly. "Well, my letter

sure stirred things up in *my* household!"

Everyone laughed, but then Allison Sterling leaned forward to speak. Now in her early forties, the former Miss America still retained her wholesome beauty. "Carrie, what these women want is what every woman needs: respect in their field, no matter what that field may be. We are harassed and condemned for everything from going to law school to having babies, from trying to become astronauts to *not* having babies, from opening our own businesses to reading romances. Women seem to be fair game—simply because we're women. For centuries men have said we're frail and need men to take care of us, when all along we women have known we're not frail at all. We've nourished children, held families together, soothed hurt husbands, given to our communities, and *still* we're criticized."

Allison's brown eyes were shining. "I say go for it, ladies. I for one will be at my desk tomorrow, writing a letter to the Asquith *Express*."

A tumult of agreement broke out, and Carrie felt her heart leap inside her. She glowed as she watched these women rally to each other.

But a shadow fell over her cheer. Andrew's face appeared in her mind. She wondered what he would think. Would he say she was being disloyal? Was it wrong to believe in a cause and act on it, especially when it might affect her husband, who mattered more to her than anyone on earth?

7

"Dr. and Mrs. Oliver Birdwell are pleased to accept the kind invitation of Dr. and Mrs. Everest for dinner on Saturday, the sixteenth of March."

Carrie reread the formal acceptance written in Agatha Birdwell's flowery handwriting and felt a spasm of nervousness clutch at her stomach. Shoving the neat ivory stationery back into its envelope, she wished she could make the upcoming dinner party disappear as easily.

She sat at the breakfast table, surrounded by glossy magazines, eyeing the newest, most fashionable recipes, the examples of trendy nouvelle cuisine. Personally, Carrie didn't cotton to it. She eyed the pale strips of veal set diagonally across a large white plate, with one or two string beans, barely cooked, and two small braised onions sitting off to the side, looking, Carrie thought, as if a couple of golf balls had wandered onto the scene by mistake.

Whatever had happened to good, wholesome, hearty American meals? She supposed they had gone the way of the unfit American. Just as jogging and handball had replaced munching in front of the television, nouvelle cuisine had replaced the traditional American meal of meat and potatoes. Still, she wasn't quite sure that this new, somewhat weird style of cooking would suit the Hopewells and Birdwells. And, more important, was Alma up to it?

Carrie rested her chin in her hand and stared at the trendy dishes, frowning thoughtfully. Finally she called into the kitchen, "Alma, could you come here a second?"

Alma appeared in the doorway almost immediately, wiping her hands on her voluminous apron, smiling cheerily. "Yes, Miss Carrie?"

"Alma, I need your help. I can't figure out what to serve when the Birdwells and Hopewells come to dinner."

Alma smiled complacently, then leaned forward to peer over Carrie's shoulder at the glossy pictures. She straightened and shook her head, her face clouded with disapproval. "Oh, no, ma'am, those just won't do. I'd recommend a good crown roast of lamb with new potatoes, fresh peas with mint, a good salad and fresh greens, and a nice domestic wine." She shook her head warningly at the gourmet magazines and clucked disapprovingly. "No, Miss Carrie, this modern stuff just won't do, at least not with the Hopewells and Birdwells."

Carrie nodded falteringly. "Crown roast of lamb? Is that the thing with those little frilly paper things on the bones?"

Alma smiled tolerantly. "Yes, Miss Carrie. That's what I'm talking about."

"Well, then, it's settled," Carrie said happily, slamming the magazines shut and gathering them into a pile. "I'll just bring these back to the library and leave it to you to organize the shopping." She stopped suddenly. "Oh. But what about hors d'oeuvres?"

Alma pursed her lips, considering. "Oh, I think a slice of Brie with imported crackers, some stuffed mushrooms, and some cherry tomatoes filled with crab salad would be rather nice."

Carrie heaved a sigh of relief. "What would I do without you?"

Alma glowed under the praise. "Oh, miss, you'd do just fine."

Carrie threw down her pen and ripped the letter to pieces, relegating it to the trash barrel with ten other attempts. She heaved a sigh and sat back in her chair. Sally was handling things out front, and Carrie was comfortable in her little office, staring out the window at Asquith's main street, with its antique shops, candy stores, cheese shops, tobacconists, and "preppy" clothing stores.

She would have been content to gaze out the window for hours, but she had a job to do. And it was turning out to be more difficult than she had anticipated. Everyone at the Women's Wednesday group had promised to write a letter to the editor of the Asquith *Express*. In the heat of the moment, Carrie, too, had agreed enthusiastically. Now she sat at her desk with eleven attempts at writing the letter torn into shreds. She looked down at the blue-lined pad of paper, and it seemed to taunt her.

Where are your firmly held convictions? it seemed to ask. *Where is the woman your parents raised? The one who speaks up about baby seals and air pollution and nuclear disarmament?*

Sighing, Carrie tried to formulate an answer. "She's

married now. She's not just a single, carefree girl any longer. She has responsibilities."

The blank pad jeered, *You're copping out. You're letting your husband run your life, think for you, act for you. You're hiding behind him because it's safer there.*

Carrie's brow knit into worried lines. "That's not true! I'm not copping out. I'm thinking in a new way, as a wife now, rather than as a single person."

Miserably she stared out the window. "You see," she whispered, "if I take a stand on this women's tenure issue, it might hurt Andrew."

The pad of paper seemed to consider that, then it came back full force. *If you don't take a stand,* it warned, *you'll hurt yourself worse. You are still your own person, with your own deeply held convictions. Can you afford to let your husband turn you into an unthinking woman, afraid to act on her principles?*

Carrie put her elbows on her desk. Her head sank into her hands. Why did it have to be so difficult? Everything had been so much easier when she was single. There had been no doubts then, no second thoughts, no nagging questions. There had been only herself to consider, and speaking up about issues she believed in was second nature of her.

She smiled sadly as she remembered sitting around the kitchen table when she was just a thin slip of a girl, arguing with her parents about the right to wear blue jeans to high school. And later she had graduated to more complex questions: the role of protest on a college campus, in slums, against government and authority figures; the evils of prejudice; the controversial issue of busing children to suburban schools.

It was in her blood, dammit! Andrew had known

that when he married her. He'd laughed and held her close and rumpled her hair and said he loved the way she spoke out so bravely on any issue that riled her.

Only now the issue she wanted to speak out on affected him personally. Now she was making life difficult for him, possibly endangering his career at Asquith. He had even gone so far as to say she was being disloyal to him as his wife.

Carrie blinked back the moisture invading her eyes and stared blankly ahead. That was what hurt the most: the accusation that she was being disloyal to him. She loved him. She would never consciously do anything that might harm him. Yet, she believed in this women's tenure issue. Must she abandon her beliefs simply because she was no longer single? When a woman married, did her loyalties shift from herself to her husband? Could she no longer think for herself, act for herself?

She thought of pushing the pad of paper away, going back out into the bookstore, and forgetting the letter to the editor. It would be so easy, really. No one would notice if she didn't write that letter. No one would accuse her of being against the women's tenure issue. She had written one letter, after all, and that had clearly shown where she stood. She didn't *have* to do anything more.

Then the little voice spoke again, and she knew it wasn't just some pad of paper chiding her. All along it had been her conscience speaking, that voice from deep inside where the heart and soul lay. The voice that made a person face herself.

You have to, Carrie, it said. *If you don't, you'll have lost a part of yourself that you'll never recover. You'll become one of the nameless, faceless Everest*

*women, smiling as you pour tea, comfortable in your
secure rut. Safe.*

For long moments Carrie pondered those words;
then slowly, deliberately, she drew the pad of paper
toward her and began to write.

Over the next few days Carrie was caught up in
the whirlwind of planning her first formal dinner party.
She sat with Alma in the breakfast room, going over
the menu, choosing the right linen and china and
crystal, deciding on the flowers, the wines, the des-
sert. She felt like a child waiting for Christmas, nervous and excited at the same time.

At night, after Andrew and she had made rapturous
love, she would lie on her back and look up at the
crewel-embroidered canopy above their bed, and all
the plans would go round and round fuzzily in her
head. She would picture it all: how she would dress,
what she would say as she presented the hors d'oeuvres,
how she would sit proudly at the end of the table,
opposite Andrew, and play the part of the Everest
wife at long last, earning her guests' and Andrew's
admiration and respect. She would sparkle. Her conversation would be witty, her appearance elegant.

She frowned, reaching up to riffle her fingers
through her wayward tresses. She would have to make
an appointment at the beauty parlor—have someone
wash and set her hair and comb it out, then lacquer
it down with that spray they used, which could probably double as stonemason's mortar.

Oh, she was going to make Andrew proud of her!
She was going to show the Hopewells and the Birdwells that she was the perfect wife for Andrew. She
was, quite simply, going to knock 'em dead.

Her letter to the editor appeared in the Asquith *Express* on the morning of Friday, March 15, the day before her dinner party. In the flurry of activity surrounding the preparations for the party, Carrie had forgotten she'd even written the letter. She was reminded quite forcefully when she looked up from nibbling a croissant to find Andrew staring at her over the top of the morning paper, his face as blank as any poker player's.

Carrie smiled and leaned over, pushed the paper out of the way, and kissed him. She became suspicious when he didn't kiss her back. Slowly she straightened.

"Okay. What is it?" she asked, smiling brightly. "Did I forget to brush my teeth? Did you forget to brush *your* teeth? Are you about to tell me you have a serious, communicable disease? Are you about to tell me *I* have a serious, communicable disease?"

"You're great on one-liners."

She grinned. "Somebody around here has to be."

He tapped the newspaper. "You've done it again."

Carrie stared blankly, then the realization dawned on her, blinding her with its brilliance.

"Oh." She plopped her elbows on the table and propped her hands against her cheeks. "It's in the paper, then."

"It is."

She nodded. She had never liked Andrew's short answers. They were a source of minor irritation to her. She would have preferred a ten-minute discourse, which would allow her to plan a suitable comeback.

She nodded again. "You've read it, I suppose."

"I have."

Very short, terse, to-the-point answers. Not a good sign. "Well," she said, straightening perkily and smiling. "The timing couldn't be better, could it? The Hopewells and Birdwells will be supplied with all sorts of brilliant table talk."

"Precisely."

Her shoulders slumped. His answers were not getting any lengthier. Definitely not a good sign. "Andrew, let's talk about this like adults. Try, just once, dear, to fashion a sentence of at least five words."

He spoke quite distinctly. She imagined he might use this tone of voice on a class full of dull-witted students. "The length of my sentences has nothing to do with the topic, Caroline."

She counted busily on her fingers, then burst into a happy smile. "Thirteen words! Darling, you're improving drastically!"

Andrew folded the paper carefully, placed it on the table, and stared at her. "Carrie, I'm beginning to lose my temper."

"Ah-ha." She nodded. "I was afraid of that."

"Carrie, why is it you can't understand my feelings about these letters of yours?"

She stared at him. "I suppose because you've never really articulated your feelings, Andrew. All I know is that you feel I'm being disloyal to you by writing letters about the tenure issue at Asquith." Rapidly, very rapidly, the conversation was becoming serious. She wished she could turn around in midstream and make it a joke again.

He shook his head vigorously. "That isn't it, Carrie. That's not it at all. I just wish that once, just once, you'd let me know in advance before you light a bomb under my chair. Maybe I'd have a chance to scramble out of the way before it went off."

Carrie closed her eyes and prayed for calm. She

mustn't flare up and let her temper get the best of her. She had to listen to what Andrew was saying. Somewhere along the way she hadn't been hearing him. Still, even to this moment, she really didn't fully understand what made him so angry when he read her letters.

She opened her eyes, her face serious. "Andrew," she said gently, "I'm afraid I just don't understand why you get so angry. Tell me again, please, darling. Tell me exactly what it is about the letters that so displeases you."

"Carrie, that's just it! It isn't the letters; it's you! It's your not telling me about them! It's your—" He broke off, helpless to explain the conflict raging inside him. He let his hands fall onto the tabletop and shook his head wearily. "Never mind. I can't explain it to myself, much less to you."

Carrie stared at her husband, willing herself to see into his brain, to read his thoughts, to understand his pain. "Are you afraid you'll lose your job because of my letters?"

"Of course not."

"Then what is it? Don't you think women professors should have the same opportunities as men?"

"Of course I do!"

She leaned forward, catching his hand and rubbing her thumb over it. "Then what, darling? What *is* it?"

He stared at his plate, his expression turbulent. Watching him, Carrie thought she could finally get a glimpse of what was going on inside him, the pandemonium there, the inability to sort his feelings from his reasons. He lifted his head and looked at her.

"Carrie, I guess I just have a different view of what a marriage should be than you do. I guess I thought—"

"What?" she prompted urgently. "You thought what?"

He considered her question for a while, then answered quietly. "I thought marriage was sharing. Sharing more than a bed and breakfast. I thought it was sharing goals and aspirations and dreams." He paused, looking into her green eyes. "I guess I thought you'd share your dreams with me, not let me stumble on them in the editorial pages of the morning paper."

She tightened her grasp on his hand, as if she were afraid that if she were to let go, he might leave her forever. "I . . . I . . ." She closed her eyes, straining to understand what he had just said. Straining to see it in all its complexity, so simply expressed. Her lower lip trembled, and she fought against the tears, but they forced their way out. She looked into her husband's eyes. "Oh, Andrew, did you think I was shutting you out?"

He reached out and brushed a tear away, then groaned softly and in one motion rose and pulled her into his arms. She clung to him, shaking, frightened of what he had just expressed. Had she done that to him? Made him feel an outsider in his own marriage? Had she come so close to making him feel left out?

"Oh, darling . . ."

"Hush," he whispered, brushing away her tears with the backs of his thumbs. "Hush. I love you."

"Oh, Andrew!" Her voice broke on a sob, and she buried her head in his strong shoulder. "I love you, too. Oh, God, I love you so much, you're like air and water and bread to me."

"I know," he murmured, rocking her. "Hush. I know."

"Andrew, never, *never*, would I shut you out of

my life. I never *thought*—I never once supposed—"
She groaned and tried to wrench herself from his arms,
but he held her tighter.

"Oh, no," he said, his voice filled with warmth,
"You can't get away that easily. It's truth time."

She couldn't meet his eyes. Ashamed, she hung
her head. "But what a terrible truth," she whispered
brokenly.

He tipped up her chin with his hand, forcing her
to look into his eyes. "What happened, Caroline
Everest?" he asked gently, smiling. "Did you just find
out you're not the perfect wife?"

She nodded, large tears welling up in her eyes.
"The most imperfect," she said. "The stupidest,
densest, thickheadedest—"

"—most wonderful wife in the world," he said,
drawing her into his arms, resting his strong, square
chin atop her shining black curls. "The most beautiful.
The most cherished. Most loved. Most adored."

"Stop it," she whispered. "How can you say those
things when I've hurt you so?"

"Because, contrary to a popular belief of some
years back, love *is* having to say you're sorry—over
and over and over again. In the coming years I'll have
to say it, and so will you. Our only hope is that each
of us will have the understanding to offer forgiveness."

She raised her eyes and studied him. "And will
you forgive me?"

"I already have."

She scrutinized his face, searching every part of it
for truth. "And all along it wasn't because you were
getting flak from the department? It wasn't because

you were against my writing the letters? It was because . . ."

"Go on."

"It was because . . . I didn't talk about my letters with you?"

He nodded. "That's pretty much it, I suppose. I guess I would have liked it if you'd come to me and talked about what was going on in your life, about what those Wednesday meetings were all about. I wish you'd thought enough of my opinion that you could have shown me the letters as you were writing them." He shrugged. "I guess I just want to be more a part of your life."

She felt dazed. Slowly she reached behind her, found her chair, and lowered herself into it. "All along I've been thinking you wanted to . . . to own me."

He whooped with laughter. "Own *you?* King Kong would have trouble handling you. He wouldn't have gotten above the first floor of the Empire State Building with you in tow."

Her green eyes took on a flash of spirit. "Just what does *that* mean?"

He grinned his wonderful, crooked grin, and Carrie felt her heart trip over itself.

"It means, my dear, that you're your own person, and any man fool enough to want to change that wouldn't deserve you. I fell in love with you the way you are, and I don't want you to change a hair on your head. I just want you to let me into your thoughts. Once in a while. Tell me what you're thinking. Share with me."

Carrie nodded thoughtfully. "You know, I think we've been coming at this thing from two different angles—me wondering how I can keep my individuality in marriage, and you wondering how to accommodate yourself to another person."

He nodded, drawing her out of her chair and into his arms again. "I'd say that's a pretty fair assessment." He lowered his lips and kissed her gently, but as he did, their bodies seemed to come alive. She entwined her arms around his neck and opened her lips. He pulled her closer, his arms tightening urgently as his tongue entered her mouth to find hers and stroke back and forth along its velvety length. Finally they parted, breath intermingling as their lips hovered millimeters apart.

"Hey," Carrie whispered huskily, "wanna cut your eight-o'clock class?"

He grinned and kissed her swiftly. "I'd love to. I'm afraid my students wouldn't like it, though."

She smiled enticingly. "Wanna bet?" She reached up and pulled at the elegant knot of his imported silk tie. "Let's conduct an experiment. Let's go back upstairs to bed and see how many students call because they worried when you didn't show up for class."

He laughed, although to Carrie it sounded more like a sexy, throaty growl. "You're a tease, you know that?"

She unbuttoned the top button of his immaculate white starched shirt. "I know. It's a liability."

Andy shook his head. "Uh-uh. I'd call it an asset."

"Picky, picky," she purred. "Always quibbling."

Her nimble fingers made fast work of the next two buttons, and Andy sighed with exaggerated patience. "Oh, very well. Have it your way. Take me upstairs and ravish me."

She smiled sexily. "I will. You just wait—"

At that, the door to the kitchen swung open, and Alma appeared, ashen-faced, her pudgy hand clutched to her ample stomach. Carrie and Andrew pulled apart, and if Carrie hadn't been so worried by Alma's appearance, she would have giggled at the way Andrew hurriedly buttoned his shirt and adjusted his tie.

It was obvious, though, that Alma hadn't noticed anything about Andrew's state of dress or undress. She looked as if she might faint. Carrie hurried forward and put an arm around her.

"What is it, Alma? Are you sick?"

"Oh, Miss Carrie," Alma moaned, then closed her eyes as if hit by a spasm of pain. "Oh, Miss Carrie, I thought it was just a silly stomachache and it would go away, only it didn't. It almost made me sick to my stomach to cook breakfast, and the smell of the food is making me ill."

Carrie and Andrew gently led her to the study and guided her to the couch.

"Can you lie down, Alma?" Andrew asked, his voice low with concern.

Alma nodded uncertainly, then shook her head and perched on the edge of the couch. "No. I feel better this way. I feel so sick. It's this horrible pain, right here, Mr. Andy."

Andrew looked up, his gazing meeting Carrie's across the top of Alma's graying head. "I'll call the doctor," he said. "You stay with Alma and see that she's comfortable."

Carrie nodded, then slipped down beside Alma and took one of the cook's hands in hers. "Where does it hurt, Alma?"

Alma clutched her belly near the waistline. "Right about here. It's been terrible, Miss Carrie, but I've been trying to pretend it's not there."

Carrie patted her hand. "Don't ever pretend again, Alma. Tell Andrew and me. We'll see to it that you're taken care of."

She looked up and questioned Andrew silently when he appeared in the doorway. "The doctor will be here any moment," he said. "And the ambulance, too. They're bringing you to the hospital for an examination, Alma. Just hold on."

Over Alma's head, Carrie's and Andrew's gazes locked. "Appendicitis?" she mouthed.

He shrugged, ran a distracted hand back through his hair, and nodded. "Looks that way," he said.

Alma was in the recovery room four hours later when it hit Carrie that tomorrow night was her first formal dinner, and that she suddenly had no cook.

8

SO MUCH FOR getting her hair done, a manicure, a pedicure, soaking in a hot tub, dressing in a leisurely manner, and assuring herself that her hair was perfect, her makeup flawless.

Instead of indulging herself in any ablutions, Carrie stood in the kitchen, staring down at the crown roast of lamb, then transferring her attention to the cookbook that allegedly told her how to prepare it. Carrie's forehead wrinkled in concentration as she reread the instructions, but all the while she was remembering her mother's words of advice on entertaining: "Never try out a new recipe on guests, Carrie—it'll fail every time."

So what was so difficult about a crown roast of lamb? You put a few garlic cloves in the meat and flavored it with rosemary, salt and papper, and then...Carrie frowned at the directions. Here they began to get confusing. To keep its shape, you stuffed it with foil and put foil on the end tips of the bones...

Carrie gnawed on her lower lip. But what about those cute little paper frills? When did they come in? In a frantic search in a gourmet shop in Asquith, she had found the paper frills and felt as if she had discovered gold. She hadn't been able to imagine sitting at the kitchen table and cutting those silly things out of paper, then gluing or Scotch-taping them together. And if one *did* do it that way, wouldn't the glue or Scotch tape be some sort of fire hazard?

Sighing, Carrie began slicing neat little slivers into the meaty portion of the lamb and inserting small pieces of garlic into the slots. Then she eyed the clock and realized it was getting alarmingly close to the time she had to go upstairs and change. She ran her eyes over her checklist once more and saw to her relief that the tomatoes were filled with the crabmeat mixture, the mushrooms were stuffed and waiting to be heated, and the Brie was softening nicely.

Inserting the last of the garlic into place, she rubbed the salt, pepper, and rosemary into the meat before shoving it into the refrigerator. It would wait until the appointed time to go into the oven along with the new potatoes, which were already peeled and waiting.

Carrie sped into the dining room, running her gaze over the table. The formal Wedgwood—as opposed to the informal, breakfast Wedgwood—was in place, the crystal water and wine goblets shining, the antique Everest sterling glowing at each place. White tapers were ready to be lit, and a bowl of white and salmon orchids graced the center of the table. They had cost the earth, but Carrie felt they were worth it.

Her glance wandered to the fireplace, and she wondered whether to light a fire. It was mid-March, and there was still a considerable nip in the air. A fire might add a nice touch.

Undecided, she waved away the thought of building a fire and raced upstairs, unbuttoning and unzipping as she went. In the bedroom she quickly divested herself of her clothes, flinging them around the room as she hurriedly found fresh underwear and pulled her simple black crepe sheath out of the closet. It was the essence of understated chic. With Andrew's mother's pearls at her throat, she thought no one in Asquith could say she didn't look the part of the gracious hostess — not even the spectral presences of Andrew's grandmother and mother, who, Carrie was sure, were somewhere in the house, unseen, watching every move she made.

Stuffing her hair into a shower cap, Carrie turned on the water and stepped under the blazing hot spray. Yelping, cringing in the farthest corner of the tub, she gingerly reached around the steaming spray and adjusted it, then slid under the now warm water and let her cares slide away. She closed her eyes in ecstasy and breathed deeply. Oh, Lord, what had the frontierswomen done without showers?

At that moment the shower curtain was shoved back, and she opened her eyes in alarm, only to find Andrew grinning at her, his tie dangling at half-mast, his hair ruffled by the March breeze.

"Want some company?" he asked amiably.

"Not on your life," she retorted, turning off the water and stepping out of the tub, then grabbing a huge, fluffy towel before Andrew could catch her. "Stay back," she shrieked, holding him off with the towel, laughing and serious at the same time. "Back! Back! I'll get a chair and a whip if you don't get back in your cage!"

Andrew leered. "A whip?"

Eyeing him sardonically, she backed out of the bathroom and rubbed herself dry. "Just undress and take a shower and get into your most dashing suit."

She glanced at the clock on her bedside table. "Ye gods! They'll be here in forty-five minutes!"

"You know, you never did tell me who's coming," Andrew said, unbuttoning his shirt and pulling it from his trousers.

Momentarily, Carrie was sidetracked from the conversation. Her eyes were mesmerized by the slowly exposed display of masculine flesh with its fine hair on that nicely muscles chest. "Oh . . ." She blinked, and pulled on her bikini panties. "Well, the Hopewells—Larry and Marjorie and Constance—"

"Constance?" Andrew interrupted, staring at Carrie incredulously.

Carrie stared back, unperturbed. "Yes, Constance. I met her at the bookstore and liked her and decided it would be foolish to live here for the next forty years and avoid her simply because she once wanted to marry you."

"You knew?"

"Well, of course I knew!" Carrie fastened her black lace bra and shrugged a complacent shoulder in Andrew's direction. "And I've been wondering about that—how come you didn't marry her?"

Andrew seemed to consider that, lips pursed; then he sighed as he sat down on the bed and removed his shoes. "Constance is nice. She's intelligent. She's sincere. She's also . . ." Andrew shrugged and let a shoe drop. "She's rather more like a sister to me than a woman. I mean, I just never loved her—not in that way."

"What way?" Entranced by the conversation, Carrie stood in bra and panties, her silken nylons clutched in her hands as she stared at her husband.

He smiled. "In the way I love you. I never felt my

heart stop with Constance. Never had the least urge to go to bed with her—or even kiss her, for that matter." He shrugged again. "I guess I didn't love her because she wasn't you."

A slow, soft smile spread over Carrie's features as she stood staring mistily at her husband. "You know something?" she asked breathily. "You have the nicest way of saying things."

He grinned and stood up, unzipping his trousers and letting them drop to the floor. "Get that dress on, woman, or we'll both be embarrassed at being caught in the act when our guests arrive." He cocked his head. "So go on. Who else is coming?"

Carrie waved a negligent hand as she sat on the bed and drew the sheer nylons up her long legs. "Just the Birdwells and Nathan."

There was complete silence in the room. Puzzled that Andrew hadn't commented on the other guests, she looked up to find him staring at her, a look of horror on his face.

"Oh, no," he said, shaking his head slowly. "You didn't. Say you didn't."

She looked at him, wide-eyed. "I did." She looked away, then looked back. "What'd I do?"

Andrew groaned, dropping onto the bed next to her. "You invited Constance, and you invited Nathan."

Carrie stared at him. "You're quite good, Andy. Your memory is awe-inspiring. I bet you'd make a wonderful witness in court." She felt her temper rising. "Now will you tell me what the hell I did?"

He held up his hands placatingly. "Hey, it's okay, all right? It's okay. No big deal. So Nathan and Constance hate each other. So what? They're adults. They can behave in public for an hour or two."

Carrie groaned, letting her body drop back onto the bed. She stared up at the canopy, that very same canopy that had listened to her nighttime daydreams about what a wonderful hostess she was going to be, and about how proud she'd make Andrew.

"How was I to know?" she asked. "who would ever expect Nathan Ridley and Constance Hopewell to hate each other?"

She sat up, intrigued. "Why *do* they hate each other?"

Andrew sighed, rubbing his chin. "Personality conflict, I guess. Nathan's a little irreverent, you know, and Constance is...Constance is a real lady. One doesn't swear in front of Constance, or tell off-color stories. Nathan realized that early on and made a practice of shocking her whenever he could. Constance just gets very quiet and raises her haughty little chin ten inches or so and pretends Nathan doesn't exist. Which of course goads him on even more." He grinned, lay back, and pulled Carrie into his arms.

"Hey," he whispered, stroking her chin with his thumb. "Who cares? It'll make for an interesting evening."

Carrie stared balefully into her husband's gray eyes. "I feel stupid."

"Don't."

"I feel like an idiot."

"Don't."

Her gaze dropped down to his chest and then returned to his face. "I feel sexy," she said huskily.

He groaned, heaving himself up. "Don't." He indicated the clock. "The clock ticketh."

She laid a hand over her heart. "This ticketh, too.

For you." Then she grinned, and they broke into laughter. "Try saying that ten times," she yelled after him, still laughing as he threw off his shirt, his undershirt, and his briefs and made for the shower.

"This ticketh, too," he shouted over the spray of the shower. "This ticketh, too. This ticketh, too..."

Crumpled up with laughter, Carrie made it to the door and slammed it shut on his litany. From the bathroom came a roar: "This ticketh, too!"

Collapsing against the door, Carrie gave herself up to helpless laughter. Pressing her hand to her lips, she dashed to the bed, picked up her dress, and slid into it. In the bathroom Andy was still chanting, undaunted, "This ticketh, too!"

Occasionally, Carrie remembered, there were contests in which the winner got the chance to run around a supermarket and gather whatever he or she could in five minutes. That's how she felt in the kitchen five minutes later. She ran from refrigerator to stove to sink, back to refrigerator, on to the stove, over to the cookbook, back to the refrigerator, all the while her heart hammering in her breast.

This time it wasn't sex that made her heart tick; it was fear. Stark, primal fear. What if she goofed up? How could she? She'd made a list and checked it twice...

"Gonna find out who's naughty or nice," Carrie sang under her breath, cradling the crown roast of lamb as she stood in the center of the kitchen, wondering what to do next. She put the roast down and raced to the stove, peering into the oven to see if the mushrooms were sizzling yet.

She glanced up at the clock. Five minutes and

they'd be here. Unless they were going to be fashionably late. Dammit, if they were, it would throw her entire schedule off. And what about the mushrooms? They were ready, and she couldn't let them get cold. Racing to the small pantry off the kitchen, Carrie searched for a warming tray. She found one in under two minutes, plugged it in, took the mushrooms out, and placed them delicately on the heated surface, then raced back to the oven to adjust it to the correct temperature for the roast.

"Twenty minutes," she read out loud from the cookbook. then she'd put the potatoes in to brown along with the meat. That would leave her the peas to cook and the cavity of the roast to fill just before she served dinner. She had already made up the salad and was pleased with her concoction of spinach, mandarin orange slices, and coconut dressing, with sliced almonds as a garnish.

The parsley, which would be daintily placed on each plate, was waiting in its little plastic bag. "Color," her mother had always cautioned her. "You can't have a decent meal if it doesn't look appetizing. Always remember to serve vegetables of different colors. It makes the plate look more attractive."

She nodded to herself, checking off yet another task performed, then raced to the refrigerator to take out the cherry tomatoes. For the next few minutes she busied herself arranging them on an attractive serving tray. Then it happened. The dreaded doorbell rang.

Swallowing, she straightened, took a deep breath, and smoothed her dress over her flat stomach and hips. Feeling about as nervous as the young Victoria must have when she was crowned queen of England, Carrie went to the door. The three Hopewells stood waiting.

From that moment on her nervousness vanished. Her own natural friendliness came to her rescue. She took their coats, chatting all the while, setting the Hopewells at ease and ushering them into the formal living room. They were just taking seats when Andrew came in, and Carrie turned to him gratefully. "Would you make drinks, darling? I've got to hurry back to get the hors d'oeuvres."

Marjorie Hopewell spoke up. "Don't tell me *you*'re cooking? Where's Alma?"

Carrie sighed ruefully. "I'm afraid she's in the hospital, recuperating from an emergency appendectomy last night."

Marjorie Hopewell's well-bred, refined face changed from polite interest to real concern. "Oh, my goodness! How terrible for you. May I help? I can go with you and—"

Carrie laughed warmly, holding up a hand. "It's lovely of you to offer, but you just sit there. It won't take a minute. I'm used to doing my own cooking, you know. It was only by the good fortune of marrying Andrew that I procured the services of a cook." She glanced at Constance, whose pale beauty was enhanced by a pink dress of fine wool, and Carrie smiled. Constance returned her smile with astonishing warmth, and Carrie hurried from the room.

"I'm used to doing my own cooking," she mocked herself under her breath. "Little Miss Perfection, the Happy Housemaker of the Year." Why couldn't she have admitted that her entertaining had been limited to spaghetti and meatballs, pizza, or large crocks of chili? This kind of elegant, formal entertaining was out of her league.

She picked up the platter of stuffed cherry tomatoes

and glared at it. Dammit, she didn't even like crab-meat!

She hurried back to the living room, set down the platter, exchanged hurried pleasantries, heard the doorbell ring, and raced to the door, color flaming high in her cheekbones from her exertions.

The Birdwells stared straight ahead, looking remarkably like the couple depicted in Grant Wood's *American Gothic*. Oliver lacked only the upheld pitchfork to complete the picture. His unwavering Yankee eyes looked out from behind wire-rimmed spectacles, and his fading black hair was carefully combed over his bald spot. Next to him, Agatha Birdwell was as unsmiling as her husband. Her eyes had faded to a dull blue, and she wore her graying hair pulled severely back into a bun at the back of her scrawny neck. She wore a plain black cloth coat that Carrie estimated had seen the last two world wars, and she held an ancient alligator pocketbook clasped to her bosom as if she carried her fortune in it and wouldn't be parted from it for the world.

Carrie pasted a welcoming smile on her face and invited the Birdwells in.

"Damn cold out there for mid-March," Oliver Birdwell said ungraciously. "Hope you have the heat on."

Carrie kept right on smiling. The worst insult on earth wouldn't faze her, she vowed. "Oh, yes!" She laughed. "We keep it on till May, if necessary."

Oliver *harrumph*ed and gave her his coat, then turned to help Agatha with hers. "Collar's fraying, Aggie," he said gruffly. "Time to get the seamstress to mend it."

Carrie turned into the closet, and immediately her smile changed to a definite gritting of her teeth. The old buzzard! Carrie couldn't help noticing that Oliver had shoved his coat toward her first, and only then had thought of helping his wife. And *his* coat, Carrie saw, was of luxurious camel hair with leather buttons, and looked as if he had gotten it that Christmas. Yet, he relegated his wife to the ragbag!

Forcing another smile, Carrie turned around, took the coat from Oliver's hands, and smiled warmly at Agatha. "I'm so glad you could come to dinner," she said. "I've wanted the chance to get to know Andrew's colleagues and their wives."

Agatha lowered her pale eyes. "We really should have invited you and Andrew—"

"Nonsense!" Oliver snapped. "He's junior faculty. It's his place to entertain us." With that, Oliver marched into the living room, leaving Agatha staring red-faced into Carrie's eyes.

"You'll have to pardon Oliver," Agatha said, color staining her cheeks. "He's . . . well, he's a little set in his ways."

Carrie felt a wave of sympathy wash over her. The poor woman! What she'd had to put up with all these years! Why in God's name had she done it? Surely she couldn't love that little oaf.

She took Agatha Birdwell's arm and gently pressed it in comradeship. Agatha, whether she knew it or not, was a perfect candidate for the Women's Wednesday group. She had obviously lived in the shadow of Oliver so long, she had become almost a shadow herself.

Leaving Agatha in Andrew's capable hands, Carrie raced back to the kitchen, unplugged the warming tray, deposited the mushrooms onto a serving tray, and began to race back to the living room. Midway across the kitchen, she remembered the roast. She'd forgotten to put the roast in! Hurriedly she put down the mushrooms and picked up the roast, her head spinning.

"Twenty minutes," she said, closing her eyes momentarily as she recalled the instructions in the cookbook. Then she would put the potatoes in.

She opened the door to the oven and was about to shove the roast in when she remembered those ridiculous little paper frills that went on the bones. Dammit, she'd almost forgotten!

Heart racing, head reeling, she felt her fingers shake as she popped the frills onto the roast and shoved it into the oven. Taking a deep breath, she ran for the mushrooms, only to skid to a halt. The timer! Twenty minutes. Twenty minutes and she'd put the potatoes in. She set the timer, rechecked that the oven was set to 475, then heaved a sigh of relief. All was well. From now on she would be able to sit down and play the role of gracious hostess.

She had the mushrooms in hand when she remembered the Brie and imported crackers. "Horse hockey!" she mumbled miserably and ran into the pantry to find a tray large enough to carry everything into the living room.

Finally she was ready. She pasted a serene smile on her face and walked sedately into the living room, beaming at her assembled guests as she placed the hors d'oeuvres on the coffee table. At that precise moment the doorbell rang, and her heart sank. She stole a look at Constance, whose head was tipped to the side as if she were listening with great interest. Constance smiled at Carrie.

"Is there someone else coming?" she asked, a becoming blush rising in her cheeks.

Carrie clasped her hands together and nodded energetically. "Yes! You're going to love him! He's just so totally . . . totally . . ." She looked toward Andrew for help, but he merely grinned into his drink and left her to invention. "Well, just wait and see who it is," she said, and she raced from the living room and flung open the front door.

Nathan was leaning against the doorjamb, his blue and crimson Asquith scarf swung nattily around his neck, his mop of curls frizzing around his head like a halo. His wire-rimmed glasses were smeared beyond belief, and Carrie momentarily wondered how he'd found his way. Surely he hadn't driven with glasses that dirty!

"What are you staring at?" Nathan asked, grinning lazily. "Are you just now realizing the mistake you made in marrying Andy and not me?"

Carrie pulled Nathan in and slammed the door shut. "I was thinking that you must have radar to find your way here with those glasses!"

She tore them off his face and began to wipe them briskly on the hem of her dress. Holding them up, she peered through them and shrugged. "Well, I suppose this is better than before."

Nathan took the glasses and slipped them on, then pretended huge surprise. "My God, Carrie! You have *green* eyes! I always thought they were slimy gray."

"Nathan," said Carrie grimly, "you're impossible." She took his coat and waited as he unwound his scarf. "Now, Nathan, listen to me. This is important."

He put his hands up behind his ears and bent them forward. "I'm all ears."

She gave a pained smile. "Look, I've gone and

done a very dumb thing, and you've got to rescue me."

"You invited the Hopewells and Birdwells to dinner, and you expect *me* to rescue you? Darling, I'll be asleep and snoring before the soup course is finished."

Soup! She'd forgotten soup! Oh, well, she'd do soup another night. Right now she had to try to smooth over her social faux pas. "Nathan, listen to me: I've invited Constance Hope—"

"What?" Nathan screamed, staring like a madman.

Carrie leaped up and held her hand over his mouth. "Now you listen to me, Nathan Ridley," she whispered in a fierce tone. "You act up in any way, and you're dead. Is that clear? No funny business. Act as if you like Constance."

He mumbled something behind her hand, and she eyed him dangerously. "All right, Nathan. I'm going to take my hand away. If you scream again, I'll kick you out that door so fast your curls will wilt."

She took her hand away slowly, ready at the slightest provocation to slam it over Nathan's mouth again. But Nathan merely twisted uncomfortably and adjusted the knot of his tie. "All right," he said, nodding slowly. "I'll do it on one condition."

"What?"

"You do my laundry for a month."

She stuck out her hand and shook his. "Agreed." Then she pushed him into the living room and beamed at everyone. "Here's our last guest, everyone! Nathan Ridley!"

There was polite chatter, the murmur of voices, the slight confusion of Larry Hopewell and Ollie Birdwell rising from their chairs and shaking Nathan's hand. Then Carrie dared to look at Constance.

She sat in her chair, wooden-faced, staring at Nathan with obvious distaste. But Nathan wasn't to be deterred. He approached her chair, took her hand, bowed over it, then brought it to his lips and kissed it slowly.

"Constance," he said, putting a hand over his heart. "My secret is out. I arranged all this. I've loved you for years from the sidelines." Going down on one knee, he grabbed her hand and held it to his heart. "Will you marry me, Constance?"

Then the smoke alarm went off.

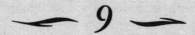

9

THE KITCHEN WAS filled with smoke as the alarm pealed, and everyone clustered in the doorway, shouting suggestions.

"Get the fire extinguisher!"

"We don't *have* a fire extinguisher!"

"What's on fire?"

"The damn roast!" snarled Carrie, not even bothering to determine who was firing the questions at her.

"Oh," said Oliver Birdwell happily, "we're having a roast?"

Carrie closed her eyes, prayed for calm, then shepherded her guests out of the kitchen. "Please, everyone, just go back to the living room. I'll take care of things."

"You already have," said Nathan, grinning snidely.

Yet, it was Nathan who guided everyone back to the living room while Andrew ran around opening windows and Carry rushed to the stove and turned it off. Coughing, she stared miserably at Andrew.

"Something went wrong," she said, eyes large and growing moist.

Andrew put a comforting arm around her and

sighed. "It's not the end of the world, honey."

"No," she said, staring at the stove, from which smoke was still streaming. "It's the end of the roast."

Shrugging, she bent and opened the door and was sent sprawling back by a cloud of black smoke. Small spurts of flames broke out as the air filled the oven; then Andy was dragging the roast from the oven, rushing it out the door, and throwing it onto the driveway. Quickly the fire went out. Carrie closed the oven door and put on the range hood to clear the kitchen of some of the smoky air. She then leaned out the window and stared at the sodden, blackened lump that was to have been dinner.

Andrew came in and put his arm around her again. "Do you have any theories on what happened? Self-immolation, perhaps? A dreaded fear of being served on the Everest Wedgwood?"

"It's the damn little paper frills," she said, nodding knowingly. "I guess you're supposed to put them on *after* the roast is cooked."

Andrew nodded. "I see. And you put them on before?"

She nodded glumly, chin supported by her hand, her elbows resting on the windowsill. "Yup. I was so churned up trying to get everything done on time that I got confused."

She turned her head and eyed Andrew. She was harboring a fear that even she didn't want to confront. It was bad enough to make an ass of herself in front of their guests, but to make an ass of Andrew! What would they all think? They'd pity him for marrying some harum-scarum know-nothing while all the while Constance Hopewell sat serenely in the living room, munching on cherry tomatoes filled with crabmeat.

Swallowing, Carrie felt tears threaten to erupt. She felt so foolish. So embarrassed. Oh, Lord, she thought, couldn't you at least open up a place in hell and let me descend?

Then she felt Andrew's arm come around her, and she couldn't muffle her fears any longer. Turning into his arms, she pressed her face into his tweed jacket. "Oh, Andrew!"

He lifted her face from his chest and dabbed away her tears. "Hush," he soothed, smiling. "Someday we'll tell our kids about it, and we'll all laugh."

"No one's laughing now," she wailed, nodding toward the living room. "Except them." She sniffled and rubbed the back of her hand across her nose. "At me."

He gathered her into his embrace and rocked her back and forth, gently murmuring to her while her tears subsided. Finally she let out a huge sigh, pushed out of his arms, wiped her mascara-stained cheeks with the palms of her hands, and summoned a smile. "Well!" she said, lifting her chin staunchly. "Dinner must go on." She looked around the kitchen, which was beginning to empty of smoke, and sighed again. "Oh, Lord. All I'm good at is spaghetti and chili and fried chicken."

"So? Make one of those."

She stared at Andy incredulously. "And serve it on the Everest Wedgwood?" She shook her head and immediately crossed the room to the pantry, taking note of its contents. Then she checked the refrigerator, slammed the door shut, found an apron, tied it on, and smiled. "You go entertain the guests. *I*'m going to cook dinner."

Smiling, Andy leaned over and kissed her nose.

"Wipe your face first, pumpkin. You look like a clown with all that mascara and soot all over you."

Horrified, Carrie clutched at her cheeks. "Omigod! Did they see me like this?"

Chuckling, Andrew told her that they hadn't, kissed her again, saluted, then left via the swinging door. Carrie hurried to the small lavatory off the kitchen, repaired her face, then set about fixing dinner.

Forty-five minutes later they all sat down to shrimp and scallops in a light lobster sauce, served in pastry shells—all taken from the freezer—with the freshly cooked peas, the salad, and a crisp California white wine.

"My goodness!" Marjorie Hopewell enthused, "however did you do it? And at a moment's notice! I'd have been devastated!"

Carrie felt a rush of gratitude to Marjorie. Carrie had thought her stuffy and too refined. Now she saw that Marjorie was rather appealing—at least when she wasn't being dominated by her husband, Larry.

"Well," Larry boomed, smiling patronizingly. "Carrie may be able to handle a domestic crisis, but she *creates* crises at the university with those dreadful letters of hers!"

Complete silence descended. Carrie's fork paused in midair, her eyes fastened on it. Marjorie Hopewell seemed to shrink in her chair, as did Agatha Birdwell and Constance. Only Oliver Birdwell straightened, nodding vigorously, shaking his fork at Carrie.

"Damned right, girl. Stirring up a heap of trouble that you have no business in. Best to stay home and cook meals and make babies."

Astounded, Carrie raised flashing eyes and confronted Ollie Birdwell. "That is the most astonishingly chauvinistic statement I've heard in my entire life!"

Oliver Birdwell waved his fork negatingly. "Chauvinistic! My Lord, I hate how you women use that term!"

Carrie's chin lifted to a defiant angle. She looked down the long length of the elegant table to see that Andrew was observing the interchange with cool interest. With a face like that, Carrie thought belligerently, he'd win any poker game he played!

"Oliver," Carrie said quietly, "have you ever wondered what your life might have been like had you been denied tenure here at Asquith?"

Oliver laughed, Carrie observed, with the nasal intonation of a hyena. "Oh!" He waved his fork again. "Never happen! I was too well qualified. I was assured tenure from the beginning."

Carrie took a steadying breath. "Oliver, has it ever occurred to you that many of those women also have the qualifications needed?"

His laughter died, and he stared at Carrie, seemingly deprived of his ability to speak. Larry Hopewell took up the gauntlet.

"Caroline." He smiled patronizingly again. "I *may* call you Caroline, mayn't I?"

"Mayn't?" Carrie asked, staring down the table at her guest. "What a quaint term. But then, you history professors are such devils!"

He rose in his seat, his eyebrows hiked up, then he settled back down, obviously unable to decide whether to take offense.

She, too, waved her fork, feeling cavalier. "Certainly, Larry. Call me Caroline. Everyone else does."

Larry smiled and went on. "Caroline, Oliver is

merely trying to point out that you have no qualifications for judging a woman's competence. You've hopped on the bandwagon because a bunch of troublemakers have talked you into it." He turned to Andrew. "I really am glad you asked us here tonight. This gives us a chance to straighten out this little mess." He looked back at Carrie. "Now, Caroline, listen to me, child. If you want to help Andrew in his career, you mustn't rock the boat he helps paddle." Larry beamed at his figure of speech. Indicating his wife and daughter with a hand, he continued, "Look. Here they are— prime examples of womanhood. They have been the binding force in my life. They have never done a thing to hurt my standing in the university, never taken up any silly causes that might discredit me."

Majorie Hopewell picked up her linen napkin, wiped the corner of her mouth daintily, and smiled graciously at her husband. "Then perhaps we're overdue."

Astounded, Larry Hopewell could only stare, openmouthed. Constance, seated next to Nathan and mute the entire evening, also sat up. "Yes, Father. Perhaps it's time the Hopewell women entered the twentieth century."

"Well, I . . ." Larry Hopewell stared from one to the other, bewildered.

Down the table, Oliver Birdwell preened. "Well, *I*'ll never have any trouble from Agatha!"

Next to her husband, Agatha Birdwell also straightened, lifting her chin and presenting him with a frozen look. "Like hell you won't!" she snapped, then picked up her wineglass and gulped half of it down. When she set the glass back on the table, she grinned at Carrie. "Lovely dinner, Carrie. You must give me your recipes."

Carrie grinned back. "I'd be delighted, Aggie. Perhaps sometime you'll come to our women's Wednesday group, which meets at my store." She looked toward Marjorie and Constance. "And I'd love it if both of you came, also."

"Great!" the three women chorused. Then Constance spoke up. "What exactly do you do at your meetings?"

"Well," said Carrie carefully, "we're thinking of organizing a protest over the women's tenure issue at Asquith . . ." She trailed off, her eyes gleaming as she looked from Larry Hopewell to Ollie Birdwell. Both looked as if they'd swallowed castor oil.

Smiling, Carrie went on, "I do hope you'll all come."

The other three women beamed at her. "Oh, we will," Aggie exclaimed. "It sounds exciting! Will you actually picket and carry those adorable little signs?"

Carrie smiled. "Yes, Aggie, I believe we will." The women chattered cheerfully, seemingly unaware of the men's feelings.

Peering down the long length of the table, Carrie tried to judge Andrew's reaction. But he was still playing poker, giving her no clue to his feelings.

Sighing, she recognized that, as a proper hostess, she must steer the conversation back to a less controversial subject. "So, Ollie," she said, smiling graciously, "I believe Andrew told me you specialize in early Roman culture. It sounds fascinating. Could you expound?"

Could he? For fifteen minutes he did so, until Carrie glanced at her watch and interrupted to say that they would have to leave if they were to attend the Wilders lecture in half an hour.

Somehow, in the mix-up of getting on coats, Carrie ended up driving with the Hopewells, while Constance and Nathan went with Andrew. At the lecture they were also separated, seated at either end of a long row of chairs.

Carrie was hardly aware of the distinguished speaker. Her thoughts were back at her home, where she had made such a colossal mess of her first dinner party. Oh, she had managed to salvage it—only to destroy all her work by bringing up the women's tenure issue. Then she rallied. *She* hadn't been the one to bring up the controversial issue. Larry had. Still, a tremor of apprehension shuddered through her. She had planned the dinner to make amends for her earlier letter, only to have written a second that made things even worse.

So far, Andrew seemed to be taking things well, but she couldn't help worrying. How had he really reacted to her failure as a hostess? Was he as ashamed of her as she was of herself?

Pretending she had something in her eye, Carrie dabbed at the tears that welled up and whispered a prayer. "Help us," she prayed. "Help Andrew and me and our marriage. We are all so frail, and it so very, very easy to make mistakes."

After the lecture there was a reception for Professor Wilders at the faculty club. It was a grand old brick Federal-style building, with faded Oriental carpets, brass lamps, and leather chairs as soft and worn as gloves. The tall, mullioned windows glowed form the lamplight within. The reception room with its paneled walls lined with paintings of distinguished faculty members—Andrew's grandfather and father among

them—was lit by a brass Williamsburg chandelier.
Cherry-wood tables groaned under delicacies of every
shape and assortment. Hugh crystal punch bowls
frothed with champagne punch, as well as a non-
alcoholic fruit punch for those disinclined to imbibe.

Carrie was inclined to imbibe, as was Andrew, she
noted. They had left the auditorium together, but there
had only been time for idle chitchat with their other
guests. Now she saw that Andrew had been button-
holed by Larry Hopewell. They were standing in a
far corner. Larry's face was inches from Andrew's,
and he was obviously haranguing Andrew about something of dire consequence.

A half hour later Andrew stood alone on the unlit
terrace of the faculty club. His face was stony as he
stared across the quadrangle, the famous Asquith
quadrangle, photogaphed so many times it had also
become a national landmark. But he saw none of it.
He was going over Larry Hopewell's words.

"Look at her!" Larry had said, indicating Carrie,
who had been standing near the punch bowl with
Constance and Nathan. "Lord, Andy, when I think of
your grandmother and mother I get sick at heart. They
were ladies! My God, the dinner parties they put on!
The grace, the gentility, the refinement of those dear,
gracious ladies. And now this!" He had wiped his
forehead and gone on, greatly agitated. "She just
doesn't fit in, Andy! Would your grandmother have
burned the roast?"

Andrew cocked an eyebrow. "My grandmother
didn't know how to cook a roast," he said mildly, but
all the while he could feel the fury building up inside,

fury at Larry Hopewell and his criticism of the woman Andrew loved.

"Now, see here, boy," Larry had continued. "You've got to come to your senses! She's going to spoil things for you if you're not careful. Your name is everything, boy. Everest! As awesome as the mountain itself. You've got a history behind you as impressive as any academician in the country. And you've got a reputation to uphold. People are depending on you, Andy! For godsake, boy, don't let us down. And please, Andy, don't let down your grandfather and father."

Andrew clenched his fists as he remembered his rage. He had twisted away from Larry Hopewell and walked angrily to the terrace, unmindful of the mid-March chill. Inside he was steaming. He felt like a caldron within, filled with feelings and impulses he had never known existed in his placid life. Now he seemed to be a stranger to himself and his heritage, filled with conflict and indecision and a strange, uncontainable yearning. At times he felt like a tiger pacing in a cage. But how could Asquith have become a cage? It was his life, dammit! He'd been born to it. But suddenly he was changing, and he didn't know if he wanted to change. And somehow, although he couldn't quite figure why, he knew the question was tied up with Carrie. She was the catalyst. When she had entered his life, he had begun to change.

Dammit!

Carrie stood at the French doors that overlooked the terrace and watched Andrew's shadowy form as he looked out over the deserted quadrangle. What was

going through his mind as he stood there, oblivious
to the dark and cold? Was he thinking of the mockery
she had made of dinner tonight? Of the embarrassment
she had heaped upon his shoulders? Was he wishing
he *had* married a woman like Constance? A woman
who fit in and didn't rock the boat?

She closed her eyes against the mist that threatened
to turn to tears, pressing her palms flat against the
cold surface of the French doors; then she shook herself and opened the doors quietly and went outside,
closing them softly behind her. Tiptoeing toward Andy,
she realized he must be lost deep in thought, for he
hadn't noticed her presence. She reached out and put
a tentative hand on his arm, and he whirled around
in surprise. Then his face relaxed, and he smiled at
her.

"You'll catch cold out here," she murmured softly,
her hand on his sleeve. She was vibrantly aware of
the feel of the fine English wool of his jacket under
her hand, intensely attuned to the scent of him—the
spice of his after shave, which, overlaid that deeper,
more intrinsic scent that was entirely him—the deep,
musky, fresh odor of his firm, strong, male body.

He reached out and drew her into his embrace. "I
at least have a wool jacket on," he protested gently.
"You're only wearing that nothing of a dress."

Carrie gazed up at him, her eyes glowing with
pleasure. "You like it?"

He smiled and drew her into his arms again. "Love
it." He sighed contentedly and rested his chin atop
her head. "Let's go home. I'm sick of this place."
His hands ran up her back, sending chills up her
spine—chills that had nothing to do with the temperature. "Anyway," he murmured, his lips grazing

her forehead and traveling toward her ear, "I have other things on my mind. You, specifically. And bed. Both together, with me making a third."

"Home," she whispered. "Yes, darling. Let's go home."

Hours later they lay together on the rumpled sheets, her head cradled on his shoulder, at rest and satisfied. They needed no words to break their contented silence. Andrew raised his hand and rubbed it lovingly over her cheek. She angled her head and smiled into his eyes.

"Love you," she said softly.

"Love you," he answered, smiling.

She turned on her side and put her arm across his brawny chest. "You make such incredible, wonderful love, Andrew. Where did you learn it?" She grinned. "Or is it just a gift, like playing tennis and squash?"

One corner of his mouth lifted wryly. "It's a gift, I guess," he said, sighing immodestly. "I guess I'm just a natural."

She punched him playfully in the side. He gathered her in his arms and held her tightly, raking his fingers through her curls.

"I should be tired," he said, "but I feel as if I could stay awake and make love to you all night."

"So who's stopping you?"

He rubbed his hand up and down the velvety surface of her back. "No one," he murmured. "I feel like king of the world right now."

She trailed her finger across his chest, twining the rough hairs around and around; then she spoke thoughtfully. "To me you are—a king, that is."

He sighed. "Who wouldn't be in this house, this

bed, this room?" He looked around, taking in the treasured antiques, the plush wall-to-wall carpeting, the drapes that shielded the windows. "Sometimes I feel as if I carry some—I don't know quite how to put it—some royal heritage, I suppose. It's the expectations, I think. At times I want to run away from it all. I want to be free of all the responsibility and the feeling that there are eyes everywhere, all looking at me, expecting great things of me." He looked down at Carrie, who remained silent, listening intently. "I have a great, burning desire to be just normal."

He sighed and lay his head back on the pillow, staring up at the canopy over their bed. "But there are so many duties, so many expectations. At times I feel so closed in by it all that I feel as if I'll smother if I don't get out from under it. I loved my grandparents and parents, but at times I wish I'd never heard of them, so that I'd have never had all this dumped in my lap—the house, the name, the profession. All the trappings of a famous, proud heritage."

Carrie rubbed her palm back and forth across his chest, listening but saying nothing. This was Andrew's time to speak, his time to let it all out. She wouldn't say I told you so, but she realized that she had from the very start seen his need, the need for air in his life. And she could bring it to him.

"You're very quiet," he said, lifting his head a little to look down at her.

She smiled. "Just listening. Understanding. Thinking how difficult it all must be for you, especially now, with me here to complicate matters for you."

He pulled her closer. "You are the best damned thing that ever happened to me, Carrie Everest." He chuckled. "But yes, you do complicate matters. Considerably."

She lay quite still and pondered his words, then raised herself up on one elbow and looked down into his face. "What do you want from me, Andrew? Do you want me to change or stay the way I am, the person you fell in love with? Do you want me to become more like your mother? Your grandmother? Do you want me to wear the right clothes and say the right things and score political points with your colleagues? What is it you want?"

He pulled her down on top of himself and cupped one breast in his strong hand. "Right now I want you to be quiet and kiss me."

She shook her head, protesting, trying to free herself from his embrace. "No, Andrew, we've got to talk about this. It's important. Our marriage hinges on it."

He shook his head. At the moment he didn't want to talk. He needed her. Needed to make love to her. To make sure she was truly his. "No," he said. "Our marriage hinges on this..." As he spoke his hands began their slow, sensual arousal, moving over her skin in magical ways, sending erotic messages to her brain, messages that tuned out the protests, the fears, the need to talk—messages that flowed through her body and heated her blood, made her feel warm and moist and ready.

She lowered her lips and kissed him, letting her lips just touch his provocatively; then her tongue darted out to lick the corners of his sensitive lips. He growled and opened his mouth over hers, letting his tongue glide out and capture hers and mate with it. His hands glided up and down her back, then dropped to cup her buttocks, the small, firm, white globes he loved so well.

She was naked in his arms, her tongue circling his with heated ardor, her hands kneading his shoulders in an ecstasy of arousal. She was warm, and her breathing was coming harder now, moist in his mouth; her nipples were hardened and pressing into his chest; her hips were moving back and forth against his aroused manhood. And he wanted her. Wanted her badly. And he was going to take her. He was going to plunge into her, hardness into softness, and plant his seed in her, so deeply that it would never be dislodged, branding her his for all time.

Almost roughly he flipped her onto her back and placed himself astride her. "Oh, God," he groaned, "I want you so much."

"And I want you, darling."

He took her then, in perhaps the most violent mating of his life. And when they lay together panting, he knew, even then, that he would take her again and yet again that night. She was a fever in his blood.

— 10 —

MARCH WAS TRUE to form: It had come in like a lion but left like a lamb. The air was filled with the promise of spring. On Asquith's manicured campus, Frisbees soared through the air like miniature flying saucers from some distant planet, the blue, yellow, and red discs swirling. Kites appeared, competing with the Frisbees for space in the balmy spring skies.

And along with April's arrival, Alma returned home. She had been hospitalized two weeks after a post-surgical infection had set in. She was welcomed with all the fuss and attention Carrie could give her.

Carrie plumped up Alma's pillows in the small, blue bedroom with its freshly washed white organdy curtains and a blue and white pieced quilt on the narrow bed. A white wicker rocking chair sat in a corner near the window that overlooked the backyard, and a vase of budding forsythia, brought in for forcing at the last moment, added a sprig of sunshine in the cheery room.

Gently, Carrie pushed the recalcitrant Alma back against the soft luxuriance of the down pillows. "There'll be no sneaking into the kitchen to make meals, Alma," she admonished firmly. "You're to rest

135

and relax and get your strength back. The doctor says you're to stay in bed most of the time for the first couple of days, then you can gradually begin getting up and walking around." Carrie pointed a firm finger at her maid. "But no work. Is that clear?"

"But I'm supposed to take care of *you!*" Alma wailed, her pudgy face red with embarrassment.

"Not when you're sick and recuperating." Carrie's face softened into a warm smile. She reached out and took Alma's thick hand. "Alma, Andrew and I care about you. We're concerned for you. After all, we've hired a temporary cook and cleaning lady, so it's not as if we're helpless."

Alma squeezed Carrie's hand. "Bless you, child. I always said when Mr. Andy brought you home that he'd brought new life into this musty old house."

Carrie grinned. "I've brought a lot more than life, Alma. I didn't want to mention this when you were in the hospital, but I ruined the big dinner I tried to cook for the Hopewells and Birdwells."

Alma lifted her hands to her eyes and peered out at Carrie through her fingers. "Omigod! You didn't!"

Carrie giggled, nodding. "It's funny now, but when it happened I was devastated. I rallied, however. I had to raid the freezer, which you had so carefully stocked, and come up with an adequate meal. Ultimately the evening was saved." A cloud came over Carrie's features. "At least gastronomically," she added grimly.

Alma looked distressed. "What happened, Miss Carrie?"

Carrie sighed tiredly and slumped onto the edge of Alma's bed. "Oh, I went and opened my big mouth and said we were planning a protest march about the women's tenure issue at Asquith, and surprisingly, Aggie Birdwell and both Marjorie and Constance Hopewell were all for it! I'm sure I sowed the seeds for two cases of severe domestic disturbance that night. I can't even begin to imagine what happened when the Hopewells and Birdwells got home."

"Serves them right!" said Alma staunchly. "The men, I mean." She shook her head disapprovingly. "They've always been such a prissy pair, ordering their wives around as if they were chattels. It sounds as if you had a good influence on Mrs. Hopewell and her daughter and that poor Agatha Birdwell." Alma sighed and lay back on her pillows. "Everyone in Asquith knows what a Tartar Ollie Birdwell is to live with. Yet, Aggie—Mrs. Birdwell, I mean—puts up with it," Alma said, blushing and looking away from Carrie's amused eyes.

"You can call her by her first name around me," Carrie said laughingly. "I'll never tell."

Alma smiled. "You know, Miss Carrie, you're a real joy."

Carrie's smile faded. "Alma, lately I've been afraid I'm more trouble than joy." She picked nervously at a button on her sleeve. "I'm beginning to wonder about myself," she continued. "I've always been so sure of myself and everything I did, but since marrying Andrew I'm not sure about anything anymore. I used to think I had all the answers, and maybe I did, just for me. But there's more than just me now. There's Andrew, too. And I sometimes wonder if I've been fair to him."

Alma frowned, then patted Carrie's hand. "Miss Carrie, I don't know much about marriage, but I've seen a few in my life, and they all have trouble sometimes. Even the best of them. Maybe from the outside looking in they seem to be all right, but on the inside, believe me, the problems are there. If you want to take the advice of an old woman who's never been married, then I'd tell you to just go on ahead and do what you feel is right. But talk about it with Mr. Andy. It seems to me, that the biggest problem in most marriages is that people don't communicate. They're afraid to talk to each other, afraid, I guess, of what the other person will say or do or think."

Carrie nodded. "Wise words," she said gently.

Alma turned her head to look out the window. "Not wise, Miss Carrie. Just my opinion, that's all. Take it for what it is—a silly old woman's thoughts on the one thing she doesn't know anything about."

Carrie studied the old, tired face in concern. "I don't know, Alma," she said gently. "A doctor doesn't have to have a disease to know about pain. A priest doesn't have to be married to counsel a married parishioner. A disinterested observer can often be more objective, so I wouldn't put myself down if I were you."

Alma turned back and smiled at Carrie. "You're a fine young lady, Miss Carrie," she said, her voice beginning to slur from fatigue. "I'm so lucky to have you here to come home to."

Carrie smiled and tucked the fresh white sheets under Alma's generous double chin. "Rest," Carrie whispered. She got up and tiptoed from the room.

The week sped by. Every night after closing Book Ends to shoppers, Carrie opened it up again to a group of elated women who brandished paintbrushes, Magic Markers, poster board, stencils, and poster paint. They knelt on the floor, laughing with the high spirits of children as they printed and painted the signs to be carried in the protest at Asquith.

Carrie sat on the floor, wearing faded overalls and a red and white checkered shirt, her curls in even more of a tumble than usual. It was her job to come up with the slogans to be used on the posters. She had already come up with the usual ones: Women of Asquith Unite—We Want Tenure; Women for Tenure—We'll Fight for Our Right. Now she gazed into space, her tongue caught between her teeth, in deep thought.

"I've got it!" she shouted, scrambling up from the floor and hushing the nine women who surrounded her.

"How's this?" she asked, eyes shining. She held out her hands as if envisioning her newest slogan: "Men at Asquith get Tenure—Women get one-ure!"

A series of groans, catcalls, and moans filled the room, followed by Magic Markers, paintbrushes, and assorted other missiles careening through the air in Carrie's direction. Laughing, Carrie shielded her head with her arms as the other women broke into laughter.

"Who gave you the job of coming up with slogans?" Louise Henderson asked good-naturedly. "You're rotten! You should be stapling posters to tomato stakes. You could probably do that all right."

Carrie grinned as she stood surveying the chaos of her usually immaculate bookstore.

Louise smiled at Carrie. "It's wonderful, isn't it?" she asked, her eyes animated. "This is how it should always be—people working together to help each other." She pointed toward Allison Sterling, her long blond hair pulled up into twin ponytails on either side of her head, her white sweatshirt spattered with paint as she joked with Irma Fahey of the history department at Asquith.

Carrie nodded. "A month ago they didn't even know each other, probably never would have met. Now look at them, laughing like schoolgirls at a pajama party."

Then her smile faded. She thought of Marjorie and Constance Hopewell, who had promised to get involved and had never shown up, and of Agatha Hopewell, who also never came to the Women's Wednesday meeting. Carrie couldn't help wondering if Marjorie and Agatha were being better wives to their husbands than she was to Andrew. Things had been so hectic lately, what with working on the protest march every night after work, and Andrew involved in his research, that they hadn't had much time to talk. While outwardly Andrew seemed to feel it was fine for her to be caught up in the protest, she wondered if secretly he resented it. That thought nagged at her, yet she hadn't been able to find the courage, much less the time, to confront him.

Louise Henderson turned to Carrie. "Hey, everything okay?"

Carrie forced a halfhearted smile. "I guess so. I don't really know. I'm beginning to wonder if I'm doing the right thing in getting so involved in this protest march."

Louise stared, obviously stunned. "Well, of course you're doing the right thing! How could you think otherwise?"

"My husband works at Asquith, remember. I keep wondering if what I'm doing will end up hurting him."

Louise nodded slowly. "Ah-ha, the plot thickens.

Are you implying that Andrew isn't behind you one hundred percent?"

"No, not at all. He seems to be all for me and what I believe in. It's just that"—Carrie sighed—"I think I'm making things difficult for him at Asquith. You know Larry Hopewell and Ollie Birdwell. They think I'm a troublemaker."

"Oh, hell." Louise dismissed Carrie's concern. "They think every woman's a troublemaker."

"Yes, but me especially, because of all this talk about Andrew's heritage, and how his grandfather and father were heads of the department, and how he's being groomed to be one someday. I know it's wearing on Andrew, but I'm not sure he'd ever say anything to me about how difficult things really are." She smiled. "I remember when I wrote those first letters, I thought he was angry at me because I wrote them and was making things rough on him at work. But really he just wanted me to share them with him, to tell him what I'd done before he discovered a letter in the paper." Her smile faded. "That's what he *said,* anyway."

"And you think he might have been lying to protect you from the truth?" Louise asked.

Carrie shuddered at the words spoken so openly. "Yes, I guess that's what I'm really afraid of. That he loves me so much that he would lie to shelter me from shouldering part of his burden—a burden *I* helped heap on him."

"Oh, dear," Louise said, "that *is* a hard one. Here you sit every night, contributing to a row at Asquith that could affect Andrew adversely. You must be consumed with guilt."

Carrie attempted to make a joke of it. "Oh! Is that

what that funny queasiness is inside me? The one that makes me feel as if little men with woolly feet are running up and down my backbone?"

"That's guilt," Louise said, grinning at her. "It's those little woolly feet that get you every time."

"Well, now I'm relieved I talked to you. I thought I had some disease or something."

Louise pushed Carrie playfully. "Carrie, I admire you. You've been a great help and a wonderful inspiration to all of us. If you're thinking of not participating in the protest march, no one will think ill of you."

Carrie heaved a sigh. "Lord, there's another worry off my back! I should talk to you more often! As a matter of fact, I *have* been thinking of that. I'm not sure whether I'll drop out or march with my placard held as high as anyone's. I just need some space to think about it—and about how it might affect Andrew and our marriage."

"Don't ever be afraid to act in your best interests, Carrie. You can't sacrifice your private life for a cause that has nothing to do with you."

"Oh, but it does!" Carrie cried. "Don't you see? That's what makes it so damn difficult! This matters, Louise, to me and every woman on earth. Just because I'm not a university professor facing a tenure fight doesn't mean it doesn't affect me. Any issue involving other women automatically involves me. If I don't help others, how can I expect others to help me when I need it?"

"The Golden Rule," Louise said softly.

"Yes." Carrie stared at the women seated on the floor. "The Golden Rule. Exactly."

"Except you're in the hot seat," Louise said. "You're

faced with the decision of whom to help first—these
women, some of whom you hardly know, or Andrew,
your husband."

Carrie sighed again. "You really understand."

Louise chuckled. "I try." She sauntered off to help
with the posters. Carrie stood quietly, wondering where
it would all end. There were only nine women here
tonight, painting posters and ready to march. Nine
women against all the men of Asquith University.

Carrie's sense of humor surfaced. "Tallyho!" she
said to no one in particular, twirling her finger in the
air as if it were a lasso. It was going to be an uphill
battle, but that's what made a fight worthwhile.

Carrie arrived home a little after eleven. The house
was dark except for a light in the hall. The door to
the study was open slightly, and Carrie saw that a dim
light shone from her room. She tiptoed to the door,
pushed it open, and stood in the doorway, watching
her husband. He was seated in his wing chair by the
fireplace, a book in his lap, his reading glasses dangling from a limp hand as he slept. She stood smiling
at the picture he made, feeling her love as a rush of
affection and pride. She walked softly over the plush
carpet and knelt by his chair, not wanting to awaken
him, just wanting to watch his face in repose.

Then she felt the small dart of fear that had bothered
her in the bookstore earlier this evening. Was he hiding his feelings from her? Was he letting her charge
willy-nilly up Pork Chop Hill in what he thought was
a foolish battle?

She looked down and saw the book he had been
reading. Curious, she leaned over and read the title.
How and When to Make a Mid-Life Career Change.

Startled, Carrie lifted frightened eyes to Andrew. Oh, Lord. Was he thinking of leaving Asquith because of her? Because she had caused him so much trouble? Was he giving up everything his family had worked for—three generations of Everests on the Asquith faculty—simply because she had opened her big mouth and made things uncomfortable for him? Was there no limit to this man's love? Would he sacrifice *all* for her?

She looked away, filled with conflict and guilt. What had she ever given up for Andrew? She racked her brain and could come up with no answer. Instead she seemed constantly to demand his attention, his understanding, his good humor. Always *he* had to understand *her* feelings. She was startled to realize that she had been essentially selfish in their relationship. Barging into the Everest home and changing routines that had become proud rituals, sweeping out the old, bringing in the new, never thinking of what the changes might mean to Andrew, of how they might affect him. No, she had her vision that Andrew's life was stifling, and so she had come to the rescue, humanitarian that she as, supposing she had all the answers.

Perhaps, she realized reluctantly, she had none of the answers. Perhaps she had been foolish and stubborn, a regular bull in a china shop, overthrowing everything Andrew had ever valued in his life. And now it seemed he was even considering leaving Asquith for another job. Another horrible thought popped into her mind: Was Andrew's tenure in jeopardy because of her activism? She lowered her head and sank miserably against the wing chair, resting her head against its side, filled with regrets.

She didn't know how long she had sat huddled there by Andrew's chair when she felt his hand touch her hair. She sat up quickly and looked into his face. He must have been awake for quite some time, for his eyes were alert and he was smiling gently at her.

"Were you sleeping?" he asked quietly.

"No. I thought you were. I've just been sitting here thinking."

"About what?"

She looked at his book briefly, then looked away. "About us."

His hand fingered her tousled hair gently. "What about us?"

She stared miserably into his eyes. "Oh, Andrew, I've been so selfish."

Startled, he closed his book, set his glasses aside, and took her hands in his. "What's this? You? Selfish? Where in the world did you ever get that idea?"

She shook her head, not wanting to hear his reassurances. She didn't want them now. This was a time for telling the truth. "No, you've got to listen to me. I've done all sorts of things that were unforgivable. I've swept into your house and overturned everything without ever thinking about how you might feel. I've been selfish and arrogant and inconsiderate and—"

"Hush," he whispered, standing up and drawing her into his arms. "I don't know what happened to put you on this guilt trip, but you're way off base, Carrie. You're the most wonderful wife a man could ever want. Now, where in God's name did you get those foolish notions?"

"Just out of my head," she said, searching his eyes. "I've just been sitting here thinking of things from your point of view. I've seen how high-handed I must have seemed, how inconsiderate of your position at Asquith, when I wrote those letters and started working on this protest march."

Fretfully she pulled from his embrace and began pacing the study. "It's just that I believe in it so much. I never did anything on purpose to hurt you or make things difficult for you. I guess I just never thought about you." Upon hearing herself say those words out loud, Carrie was consumed with guilt. "Oh," she wailed. "I've been so selfish!"

With that she dissolved into tears, and Andrew took her into his arms and comforted her. "Will you stop crying?" he finally asked. "How else am I going to get you to stop all this foolish talk about being selfish?"

She sniffled, looking up at him warily through tear-misted lashes. "But I have been," she insisted.

He chuckled. "That, my dear, is a crock."

Startled, she stared at him wide-eyed, then began to giggle. He joined her in laughter, taking her in his arms once again. "That's better," he said soothingly. "I like it much better when you laugh than when you cry."

"Yeah, I've always thought it was more fun to laugh, too."

"Then let's keep that as a resolution, okay? No more tears?"

Smiling, she nodded, then watched as he bent to turn off the light. She held on to his arm. "Andrew, wait. I need to talk to you."

He turned back to her, his eyes questioning. "What's so important we can't talk about it upstairs in bed?"

"Because if we go upstairs to bed, I won't want to talk."

"Precisely," he said, laughing as he once again bent to turn off the lamp.

"No! I really have to talk to you." She waited until he turned back to her and went on, "Really. It's important."

He sighed, folded his arms, sat on the arm of his wing chair, and nodded. "Okay. Talk."

She pressed her hands together and took a few paces across the room, then turned back to him. "It's about this protest march."

"What about it?" he asked equably, showing no signs of discomfort or irritation.

She took heart from that. "Andrew, I'm not going to take part in it."

He stared at her, his face slowly growing more serious. "What?" he asked incredulously, getting up and crossing the space that separated them. He put his hands on her upper arms in gentle concern. "What's this? Not take part in it? But, Carrie, you believe in it."

She searched his eyes. "I believe in us more."

He shook his head as if trying to clear it of fog. "Wait a minute. What's 'us' got to do with the march?"

She reached out and pressed her palm against his cheek, looking up into his gray eyes, feeling her love rise up within her like a great ocean wave, overpowering in its might, awesome in its beauty. "Andrew, I believe in the issue of women's tenure, but I also believe in us. And I've had to think long and hard the past few days—tonight especially. I think there comes a time in every marriage when a person has to be willing to make a sacrifice. A big one. Not just some little thing, like settling for poached eggs when you really want scrambled. I will do everything in my power as long as I live to help women achieve equal rights, but I'm willing to give up participating in this march if it's going to hurt you. There will be other battles, battles that won't affect you, and I'll fight in those. But right now I have to step back and see where my priorities lie. I can't ask more from you than I'm willing to give myself. Marriage is a two-way street. I can't believe I'd be compromising my principles by not participating in the march. But I might be sacrificing something infinitely more precious—your trust in me. Our love. Our marriage."

Andrew stood looking into Carrie's eyes; then he gathered her in his arms with an inarticulate moan, lifting his hands to cradle her head. "Carrie, listen to me," he whispered against her ear. "I love you more than life itself. And your being willing to give up the march for me is the most profoundly beautiful gift you could ever give me. But by offering me that gift, I can give you something in return—the freedom to march in the protest."

He ran his thumb down her cheek, gazing into her rapt green eyes. "I am so damned proud of you, Carrie Everest," he said, his eyes shining. "You are everything I ever wanted in my life. And now, tonight, you've told me that I matter more to you than anything else, and that's all I need, Carrie. Just to know that you love me and value me. I would never ask you to sacrifice doing something you believe in so very much. I want you to march, honey, right there at the head of the parade." He smiled crookedly. "Knock 'em dead, princess. I'm with you all the way."

"Oh, Andrew!" She sank into his arms, her heart filled with love. Had there ever been such a wonderful man? Ever in the entire history of the world?

— 11 —

ANDREW WALKED TOWARD campus with his head down, staring at the sidewalk, remembering his conversation with Carrie last night. It had been the most moving incident of his life, to realize that Carrie loved him enough to sacrifice acting on her beliefs. But he couldn't ask that of her; that was like keeping the one you loved in chains. Real love flourished in the open, given freely, freely accepted, with no restrictions applied.

He lifted his head, feeling the wellbeing filter through to his very soul. And as he walked he began to look around, his first real look at the Asquith campus in years. Perhaps in his entire life. Asquith was so much a part of him and his life, he sometimes wondered where Andrew Everest left off and Asquith began. But now he genuinely looked at his surroundings, taking in the precisely landscaped campus, the proud old buildings with their requisite covering of ivy, the Gothic towers, the gables, the granite statues, the precise layout of sidewalks that crisscrossed the campus like gridwork, the crowds of students in their Top-Siders and designer jeans and monogrammed T-shirts and sweaters, all wearing the look of money and grace and refinement even at the tender ages of nineteen and twenty.

They were all the lucky ones, as he himself was— born into money, taking its advantages for granted. They were the ones from families who had "contacts," the ones who didn't have to worry about getting a job after graduation. They belonged to the families whose fathers were part of the old-boy network, and there would always be a place in someone's firm for them.

For the first time Andrew wondered what it would be like to have no "contacts," no monied friends, no relative with an in at the best law firm in New York or a senator's office in Washington. What was it like to have to struggle for a living? He stopped walking and stared across the impressive quadrangle, where the forsythia was bursting into bloom. *What was it like to be a woman?*

His eyes scanned the campus, taking in the laughing coeds with their shining manes of hair. He thought about Irma Fahey and Liz Dawson in the history department. He didn't know either of them very well, but he knew they came from middle-class families, had gotten their education on scholarships and through loans. They'd had to struggle for what they had attained, and now they were faced with losing it. Losing what he was virtually assured of.

"Good morning, Dr. Everest," one of his students greeted him, flashing strong white teeth beneath a mustache designed to look like Robert Redford's in *Butch Cassidy and the Sundance Kid.*

Andy snapped out of his reverie, smiled at his student, and strode toward his office. Yet he continued to take in his surroundings as he walked, remembering that night in mid-March when he had stood on the darkened terrace of the faculty club, looking out across the quadrangle, wondering why he felt caged. Now, standing on the steps of the history building, which had been named after his grandfather, he felt the same feelings return, as if iron bars were closing in on him, caging him in a world he neither wanted nor liked.

Turning, he took the granite steps two at a time, elbowing past the students, trying to banish the tightness that bound his chest. He was striding rapidly along the crowded corridor when he heard Larry Hopewell call his name. He hesitated a second, wanting more than anything to pretend he hadn't heard Larry. He wanted to find refuge in his office, joke with Nathan, then lose himself in the deadly, dry lecture he was to give on English law and society.

Instead he faced Larry, forcing a smile as Larry took him by the elbow and ushered him to a silent corner off the hallway.

"You've heard about the protest march, of course," Larry said darkly, staring at Andrew bleakly. "Your little wife seems to have spearheaded the entire mess."

Andrew rocked back on his heels, shoved his hands in his pants pockets, and grinned amiably. "My 'little wife'?" he asked, fury leashed and in control but bubbling just beneath the surface.

"Oh, Andy," Larry said, irritably waving away the rhetorical question. "This is no time to get upset over my choice of words. The point is, you've got to do something. She's a damned nuisance, running around inciting rebellion. Ollie and I were able to squash Marjorie and Agatha's silly notions of protesting; now you've got to stop Carrie. My God, Andy! I had a reporter from *The New York Times* call me for a comment on her charges that Asquith is a century behind the times!" Larry blew out a beleaguered breath. "She's dangerous. We've got to stop this silliness and have her start acting like the responsible wife of a prominent Asquith professor."

"I'm not prominent."

"Dammit, Andy, stop hedging!" Larry fumbled in his inside jacket pocket and found his leather tobacco pouch, then reached into his breast pocket and retrieved his pipe. He began packing tobacco into the pipe nervously, his eyes shifting here and there, as if there might be spies listening.

Andrew rocked back on his heels again, enjoying Larry's discomfort. "So what did you say to him?"

Larry swung his head up and stared. "To whom?"

"The reporter."

Larry cursed gruffly. "Damn cheek of the fellow! I told him Asquith is proud of its tradition and excellence in education and that only the best-qualified staff were awarded tenure. That shut him up!"

"How's the evaluation committee going? You're chairman; you must know which way the wind's blowing."

Larry shook his head worriedly. "Not good. All this publicity is beginning to worry some of the tenured people. They're saying maybe we ought to award tenure to the women and forget the entire mess."

Andrew quirked an eyebrow. "And you don't see it that way?"

Larry guffawed. "Can you see Irma Fahey tenured at Asquith? Oh, she's an intelligent woman, but my God! No connections, no social network. Comes from some small town in *Iowa,* for godsake!"

It flitted through Andrew's mind that now might be a good time to flatten Larry Hopewell, but he kept his patience. "Well, Irma's a very good scholar. Her papers are first rate. She's gotten them published in the best journals, and she's well respected in her field."

"Her *field*," Larry Hopewell sneered. "Women in history! Preposterous!"

"You have to get your head out of the sand, Larry," Andrew said, still in control. "Every major university has a women's studies department. It's here at Asquith out of tokenism, but we are lucky to have women of Irma Fahey's and Liz Dawson's qualifications."

"It's rubbish! Pure and total rubbish!" Larry puffed on his pipe angrily, then held it out and pointed it toward Andrew as he spoke vehemently. "Let me tell you a thing or two, Andrew. Your grandfather or father wouldn't have stood for it!"

"They wouldn't have had to," Andrew said mildly. "Feminism hadn't surfaced then, except in more advanced circles."

Larry stared, astounded. "Are you implying that Asquith isn't advanced?"

Andrew smiled benignly, then turned to walk away. "Yes, Larry, I am," he said over his shoulder before disappearing into the milling crowds.

In his office he threw down his briefcase and cursed vigorously. Nathan looked up from his desk and sat back, propping his hands behind his head and putting his feet up to rest on the top of his desk. "Another fight with the little wife?" he asked, beaming.

Andrew glared at him. "No, and dammit, she isn't the *little* wife! I just was talking with Larry, and that's what he insists on calling Carrie—my 'little wife,' the revolutionary." Andrew poured himself a mug of coffee and went to sit on top of the radiator—which was cold, since the heating had been turned off—and stared down on the campus.

At his desk, Nathan smiled and lowered his feet from his desktop. "All right, Andy, open up. What's bothering you?"

Andrew stared down at the students milling about the campus and shook his head. "I'm not sure. It's just a feeling I've had lately." He shook his head and began pacing around the office. "Before I met Carrie, I never questioned my place here, Nathan. You know that. Oh, we used to laugh and poke fun at Asquith, but we both loved the old place." He frowned. "At least, I always thought I did."

"And you don't any longer?"

"I don't know. Now I get the feeling that I'm in a cage, that the only time I come alive is when I leave this building and get home and see Carrie. Sometimes I'll be sitting here, correcting papers or preparing a lecture, and I'll look out that window and think of Carrie in the bookstore and wish I were there with her instead of here. I feel as if I'm a traitor at times. I was born to this, Nathan, but suddenly I don't seem to give a damn about it."

Nathan nodded. "We're brought up to believe we have a place in life, and when we grow up and realize that it's not the place *we* want—that it's what our parents wanted for us—then we're scared and mixed up and confused."

Andrew settled on the edge of his desk. "When did you get your degree in psychology that you know so much?"

Nathan grinned, flinging the pencil up in the air and catching it as it fell. "Because I know what you're going through. I've known you almost all my life, Andy, and I saw what happened when you met Carrie.

You had never questioned your place in life; then you met Carrie, and it was suddenly like seeing another, more exotic world, a world you'd never dreamed existed, a world where people laughed and made love and joked and relaxed. You come from the most traditional upbringing in America, Andy, and Carrie showed you that parts of it represent stuffiness and stale air."

"Then why do *you* stay here?"

Nathan laughed. "First of all, for me Asquith *is* the other world. I got here not out of family tradition but on a damned good brain, through scholarships. When we met at prep school, you were the only one who was friendly to me. I didn't belong, Andy. I was a little skinny Jewish kid from the Bronx, and I didn't know about salad forks and soup spoons. You took me under your wing, and I vowed that someday I'd be like you." He laughed again, sardonically. "Well, I pass now. I'm accepted here. I've lost my telltale Bronx accent, and I can be witty and charming and fit in here with all the social animals. So you see, I want what you were born to, and it turns out that you wouldn't mind having what I was born to."

Andrew stared into his coffee mug. "So what's the answer, Nathan? Should I take Carrie and run off to the Bronx and open a delicatessen?"

Nathan grinned. "I can't see that. No, I think you should follow your gut feelings, Andy. The feelings that are true to you. If you try to figure things out logically, using reason, always trying to do what's right, you make a mistake every time."

"You should be in the Student Center, counseling instead of teaching history."

Nathan merely grinned and went back to his work.

Andrew grinned, too, and sipped his coffee. "Say, who's your latest conquest, Nathan? I haven't heard you talking about any of the coeds lately."

Nathan shuffled through his papers. "No one in particular. I'm getting a little too old for all that late-night carousing."

Andrew stared at Nathan's back. Something was fishy. When Nathan sidestepped a question about the women in his life, something was up. Intrigued, Andrew slid off the edge of his desk and took a seat behind it. He sat and tapped a pencil against his teeth, wondering. Could Nathan have finally fallen for someone? Nathan, the freewheeling bachelor, who had kidded Andrew unmercifully when his whirlwind courtship with Carrie had abruptly ended in marriage? Smiling, Andrew leaned back in his chair and tried to remember whom Nathan had last dated. No one in particular came to mind. Oh, well, he'd find out sooner or later.

Late that afternoon Carrie looked up from her work to see Constance Hopewell come flying into the store, her face shining, her blue eyes glowing. Carrie stared as if at an apparition. There was something so absolutely radiant about Constance that it almost took Carrie's breath away. On closer inspection Carrie realized that Constance was wearing makeup, yet that couldn't account for the happiness that shone in her eyes.

Constance stopped at the counter and beamed at Carrie. "Carrie, can we talk?"

Carrie grinned and motioned to Sally to take over, then led Constance into her office and closed the door. She pulled a chair up next to her desk for Connie, then sat down at her desk.

"What gives? You look marvelous. Did someone discover you on campus and sign you to a movie contract?"

Constance laughed happily, shaking her head. "I . . . I don't know how to tell you, but I felt you were the only one I *could* tell. And I've just got to tell someone!"

Carrie smiled and sat forward. "Well, what is it? It must be wonderful to make you look like this."

Constance's eyes fell demurely. "He is," she whispered.

Carrie sat stock still, the words echoing in the office. "Who's *he?*"

Constance looked up, eyes glowing. "Oh, Carrie. It's Nathan."

Carrie's mouth began a slow motion smile, but when it got into high gear, she let out a war whoop of happiness. "Yaa-*hoo!*" she yelled, and reached forward to hug Constance, who hugged her back, tears trickling down her pink cheeks.

Carrie released her and grabbed her hands. "All right, all right, so tell me everything. Everything." Then she glanced at Constance's blushing cheeks and said, "Okay, *almost* everything."

"Oh, Carrie, I don't know where to start. At your house, I guess—where it all began. I could have killed you when I saw you'd fixed me up with Nathan. I'd hated Nathan—he was always so damned cheeky and teasing me all the time about being a prude. Anyway, I couldn't stand him. It was Andy I was crazy about—" She stopped, looking horrified, and put her hand to her open mouth. "Oh, Carrie, forgive me!"

Carrie waved away her words. "Hell, I knew all about that. So go on already."

Constance stared at Carrie. "You truly are the most

amazing woman," she said slowly.

Carrie grinned. "Go *on,* will you?"

"Well, as I said, at first I was just so angry to have to sit through that dinner with Nathan, of all people. I mean, to me he represented all the worst things a man could be—cocky, brilliant and well aware of it, and a skirt-chaser from the word go. But anyway, he was so kind to me that night..."

Carrie laughed to herself. He darned well should have been! Carrie was still doing his laundry for him as her part of their bargain. Of course, she'd never imagined that they'd actually fall in love! Andrew had convinced her they hated each other.

"Anyway," Constance continued, "we went to the lecture, and he was so gentle with me, as if he knew I was scared stiff about being with him. Now that I look back, I don't think I ever actually hated Nathan. He just scared me. He's so brilliant, and he always seemed to be mocking me. I know now that he was trying to tease me into loosening up a little. I could never say a word around him for fear of getting tongue-tied. Nathan is absolutely brilliant—smarter than Andy, even—" She broke off again, apparently aghast at what she'd said. She stared at Carrie, her eyes pleading for forgiveness.

Carrie merely laughed. "Just get on with it, Constance. Everyone knows Nathan is the next Einstein."

"Well, anyway, he took me out for a drink afterward at a quiet, out-of-the-way cocktail lounge, and I guess the liquor loosened my tongue, because we talked a lot. I wasn't frightened anymore, and I ended up telling Nathan a lot about myself. More perhaps than I've ever told anyone." She smiled radiantly. "Well, he took me home, and I was trembling, because I suddenly realized that more than anything, I wanted to kiss him. But he didn't. Well, I mean, he did, but not the way I wanted him to. He just leaned down and kissed me gently on the forehead and squeezed my hand and said, 'Good night, beautiful Constance.' And then he was gone, and I was standing there, just staring after him, in a confused state. I went inside and cried into my pillow because I thought I'd never see him again—or rather, that he'd never ask me out. But the very next day he stopped by the reference department in the library when I was at work, and he asked me to have dinner with him..."

Carrie sat and waited. *"And?"*

Constance blushed. "And so we began going out. And inevitably Nathan brought me back to his apartment and...well...I...couldn't..."

Carrie nodded, filled with understanding. Then Constance heaved a sigh and smiled brilliantly. "Until last night!"

At that, Carrie's face lit up. She reached out and squeezed Connie's hands. "Oh, Connie, I'm so very happy for you."

Constance nodded, beaming. "Oh, it was almost a third-rate comedy at first. I kept saying no, but my body kept saying yes, and Nathan listened to my body instead of me, and the next thing I knew, he was carrying me into his bedroom and I was scared to death, but I felt as if I were standing on heaven's doorstep all the same." She closed her eyes as if remembering, savoring it all over again. Her face became transformed, magically filled with serene beauty. "Oh, Carrie! He was so gentle! I had never imagined a man could be so gentle. And I stopped being afraid, and he stopped being quite so gentle, and . . . and . . . it happened!" She beamed at Carrie. "Oh, I am so wonderfully happy!" She hugged herself, laughing exuberantly. "Oh, Carrie, I feel so alive—as if all these years I've been packed in ice and just waiting for the right man to come along and pick the ice away. It's a thousand times more beautiful than I ever imagined it could be." Her eyes met Carrie's. "And I owe it all to you."

"I had nothing to do with it!" Carrie exclaimed, delighted. "It must have been chemistry, because when I told Andrew I'd invited Nathan as your escort, he told me how you two couldn't stand each other, and I thought I'd make a complete mess of that night. Of course the burned roast was yet to come . . ."

"Well, it turned out fantastically." Constance smiled. "And you know the most wonderful part?" Carrie shook her head. "Afterward we lay together and Nathan held me and said he loved me."

Carrie nodded. She didn't have to say anything. She and Constance understood each other perfectly. *I love you* were often the most precious words in a woman's life.

Constance broke the silence by standing up. "Well, I just had to tell you. I knew you'd understand."

Carrie stood up and hugged her. "Yes, I do. And I'm so very happy for you and Nathan."

"No one else knows, of course, especially not Mama and Daddy." Constance lowered her eyes, then raised them and looked directly into Carrie's. "Daddy still thinks Andy will divorce you and marry me."

Carrie considered that, raising her eyebrows. "He does, does he?"

Constance grinned. "I can see that doesn't sit well with you."

"Not very."

Constance laughed. "Nathan and I are getting married. I wanted you and Andy to be the first to know."

Carrie hugged her again, then watched as Constance seemed to waft from the store, floating on the wings of love.

That evening Carrie stared at the calendar, then flipped it back to March and stared at one particular date: March 16. Then she put a hand to her stomach, considering. A thoughtful frown creased her forehead when she turned from her desk to Andrew, who was reading in "his" chair. The new chair she had ordered had arrived and was now officially "hers." Andrew seemed to take special pride in having won his patriarchal chair back for himself. He appeared to be reading, but on closer inspection Carrie saw that his eyes were sliding shut and he was beginning to nod off.

She tiptoed up to his chair, expecting to see that he was falling asleep over some history tome, but realized that he'd been reading about the stock market. She stared down at the book, and it hit her that lately Andrew had been more and more interested in the market. He'd always planned his own investments, telling his broker when to buy and when to sell, but now he seemed to take an even greater interest in it. He folded the newspaper every morning to the stock market page and made copious notes that later ended up programmed into his personal computer.

She leaned down to read the title of the book in his lap: *How to Begin Your New Life as a Stockbroker*.

She straightened and thoughtfully digested that, then poked Andrew on the shoulder. "Hey, sleepyhead, time for bed."

He roused himself. "I wasn't sleeping. Just resting my eyes."

She grinned and headed for the door. "Well, I'm off to bed. Big day tomorrow." She paused on the way out and cocked her head inquisitively. "The protest march is tomorrow."

Andrew stared at her, then nodded. "Well, you go on up. I'll be up later."

Carrie didn't argue. She stepped out into the hallway and closed the door behind her, then quietly went about shutting off the lamps along the way upstairs. In her bedroom, she changed into a nightgown and sat at the vanity in the double bathroom and brushed her hair, staring at herself in the mirror.

What did Andrew really think about her marching? He'd said he wanted her to, but did he really? Was he staying downstairs because he didn't want to be with her tonight, because he really felt she was betraying him by marching?

Her questions were answered when she looked up and saw his reflection in the mirror. He stood in the doorway to the bathroom, his shirt unbuttoned, his tie dangling askew, his sleeves rolled halfway up his sinewy arms.

"Hey," he whispered. "Come here."

She turned on the stool, stood up, and walked toward him, then stood waiting. Slowly he reached out and undid the tiny bows of each shoulder that held up her nightgown, watching with evident satisfaction as the gown tumbled to the floor, leaving her naked in front of him.

"Better," he said, picking her up and carrying her to their bed. "Much better."

As he settled her into the soft mattress she smiled up into his eyes. "And this," she whispered against his lips, "is even better."

— 12 —

IN ONE WEEK the evaluation committees of each department at Asquith would make their recommendations for tenure. Then those names selected would go to the department dean, where they would be approved or disapproved, though generally official approval was a given. From there they went to the promotion and tenure committee of the entire university, and thence to the president of the university.

Today, three-quarters of the way into April, the air was balmy, the sky a robin's-egg blue with white powder-puff clouds wafting by. Television cameras and commentators were there from all the Connecticut stations and the three major networks, as well as a cable news station. Radio station crews were there in hordes, their sound equipment tangling with that of the television teams, while newspaper reporters stood about in clusters, their notebooks in hand, laughing at stale jokes as their heads swiveled to catch a possible new angle on the story.

The students were converging on the quadrangle, all thought of attending classes evidently forgotten. Small groups had brought picnic lunches and a few threw Frisbees and flew kites, while others, coeds mostly, handed out pamphlets and talked earnestly with reporters.

Andrew stood in his office window next to Nathan and shook his head admiringly. "I didn't know they had it in them," he said. "Look at that group down there. You'd think a rock star was appearing instead of a group of local women protesting Asquith's tenure policies."

Nathan grinned, his eyes scanning the crowd. "I think you're in for a surprise, Andy. Carrie has been going out organizing this thing as if she were a pro; in a quiet, thoroughly professional way. She's got every woman in Asquith fired up." He folded his arms and turned to look at Andrew. "And not a few men. I'm marching, too. Care to join me?"

Andrew's head turned so quickly he was in danger of dislocating his neck. "You *what?*"

"I'm marching."

Andrew stared, then slowly smiled. "Oh, I get it. You're dating a coed who's into this, right?"

"Not a coed, and we're not just dating. We're going to get married."

Andrew sat down quickly in his chair and let the news sink in. "Oh, my God." He looked up, then stuck out his hand and pumped Nathan's eagerly in congratulations. "Well, who is she, for godsake? Is this why you've been so quiet about women lately?"

"I suppose it is. I'm marrying . . . well, it's Constance."

Andrew stared. "Constance? Constance who?"

Nathan waited, grinning, until Andrew raised his hand to his head and stared, dumbfounded. "Hopewell. It's Constance Hopewell, isn't it?"

Nathan nodded, grinning. "Sure is. I want you to

be my best man. Connie's going to ask Carrie to be her matron of honor."

"Will this be a big wedding?"

Nathan shook his head. "Strictly civil ceremony. Constance has no desire to convert to Judaism, and since I haven't practiced it in twenty years, it seems foolish to go that route. My parents will be disappointed, of course, but when I win the Nobel prize in fifteen years they'll forgive me." Grinning, he sauntered toward the door. "Maybe I'll see you down there," he said, leaving Andrew sitting there, staring bemusedly after him.

Carrie's voice resonated through the loudspeakers, passionate in its conviction. Her hands were clenched into fists that pounded the podium to underscore her points. She was the last speaker, and the crowd stood mute, completely attuned to this woman with the impelling voice and earnest conviction. On the edge of the crowd Andrew stood watching, feeling his heart swell within him, not just with pride but with something else, something unnameable.

Standing quietly, intent, he felt the bars of his cage open, saw them fall away, as if melted by the passion in Carrie's voice. He felt as if the world was spread out before him, his for the taking. For the first time he realized what Carrie represented: freedom.

With Carrie he was no longer chained to Asquith. He was free to find his own path, to lead his own life, here or somewhere else, teaching or changing his entire life's work. Tradition, the assigned place, no longer held him in bondage. He was free, and at that moment he thought he loved Carrie so fiercely that he would never be able to communicate it to her. He wanted to push through the crowd and climb that podium and take her in his arms, away from the crowd that hung on her words. He wanted her for himself, totally, selfishly.

But then he realized he couldn't do that. Carrie was meant for this, and she belonged as much to these students as she did to him, for she gave them freedom, also. Freedom of choice, freedom to question, to tear down old buildings that were decayed and build new ones, fresh with promise.

He stood in the April breeze, feeling it ruffle his hair, and watched proudly as she ended her speech, arms raised triumphantly overhead, while the cheers roared around her and Frisbees and hats were thrown high overhead.

From somewhere a band started playing the Asquith fight song, and the crowd started singing with one voice. Andy saw a television reporter excitedly talking into his mike while the camera panned the crowd. Then it was mass confusion, as the original group of marchers were joined by the students and the quadrangle became a mass of singing bodies, all linking hands, marching together toward the fountain where the archangel Gabriel held high the scrolls of learning. The crowd ringed the fountain, hoisting Carrie and the seven women faculty members of Asquith up on the low border of the fountain. Andrew turned away then and walked silently back to Edward Haynes Everest Hall and his office.

He was stopped by Larry Hopewell, who had been staring out a window from the main hallway, his face fierce with anger. "Well, they've gone and done it now!" he snapped, falling into step beside Andrew. "We're going to be forced to give those two women

tenure, as will all the other departments." He stopped
walking and stared down at the floor, shaking his head
in disgust. "I can't stand it, Andrew. I can't stand to
see the old ways die. It's everything that makes my
life complete—the traditions here." He raised his eyes,
and Andrew saw they were filled with sadness.
"Constance was out there today, Andy. My own
daughter, Constance."

He looked down at the ground sadly, turned, and
walked off. Andrew watched, noting the defeated
slump of his shoulders. It was as if all his self-
importance had fled, replaced by sadness and defeat.

Andrew turned and made his way to his office. He
poured coffee and stood at the window, surveying the
crowd below, which was slowly beginning to dis-
perse. And as he stood there he realized what he was
seeing: history. Change. The ivied walls of Asquith
might stand for centuries more, but today a new ivy
plant had been introduced, to flourish alongside the
old ones. And one day it, too, would be old and solidly
attached to the sides of the building, and someone
else, someone young and filled with zest and new
ideas, would come and plant yet another kind of ivy.
Part of Andrew could understand the sadness Larry
Hopewell must be feeling, but he knew in his heart
that new plants had to grow. It was inevitable—
change. It was what he had once feared. For the first
time today he had recognized it as something to be
welcomed rather than feared. And there, he supposed,
lay the difference between him and Larry Hopewell.
And between him and his father and grandfather...

Two weeks later the letters arrived in Andrew's
and Nathan's office, delivered by messenger. They

stared down at the offical department stationery and fingered the envelopes.

Nathan shrugged and slit his envelope open.

"May as well see what the news is," he said, grinning.

Andrew slit open his and read, too. It said what he'd expected all along: He'd been recommended for tenure at Asquith in the history department. He looked up at Nathan and realized his friend was staring down at his letter, his grin gone, his face white.

"What's the matter, Nathan? Can't you believe you made it?"

Nathan looked up. "That's just it, Andy—I didn't."

Andrew marched along the busy corridor, his hands bunched into fists, his lips thinned in anger. He shouldered his way past students and fellow faculty members and stormed into Larry Hopewell's office. The secretary looked up and smiled, but her smile faltered when she saw the expression on Andrew's face.

"Good morning, Dr. Everest. How nice to see you." She glanced toward Larry Hopewell's closed office door and forced a smile. "Dr. Hopewell is in conference."

Andrew nodded curtly, striding toward the closed door. "Tough," he said, throwing open the door and letting it slam back against the wall. The three men seated in the office started, then stared at Andrew, whose face was filled with wrath, his hands still clenched.

"Get out," he commanded. "I want to talk with Larry."

The two men shot out of their chairs and scrambled

by Andrew, who reached out and slammed the door shut. A picture on the wall trembled momentarily, then fell silent again.

"Who got tenure?" Andrew asked without preamble.

Larry smiled heartily. "Sit down, Andy, my boy. Sit down." He opened a humidor and took out a cigar. "Let's celebrate, shall we? You made it, of course."

Andrew reached out and slapped the cigar from Larry's hands and watched as Larry followed its progress halfway across his office to where it finally bounced to a stop against a radiator.

"Who got tenure?" he asked implacably.

Larry heaved a sigh and wiped his hands on his thighs, which were encased in faded, worn corduroy.

"Well," he said, "you, of course, and Irma Fahey, and Liz Dawson."

"And Nathan?" Andrew stood ominously quiet, his tall, lean body casting a menacing shadow over Larry Hopewell.

Larry got up slowly, walked to a window, and looked out, his hands clasped behind his back. "We felt we had to give the women tenure, Andy. All that pressure and the news reporters were making us look bad. Nathan's got a brilliant future ahead of him. He doesn't need us—"

"Dammit! We need *him!*" Andrew snarled.

Larry sighed again and turned around, holding out his hands entreatingly. "Andy, you've got to understand. This was a political thing. We all think the world of Nathan, but someone had to go."

"Then why not me, dammit?" Andrew asked, pounding his chest. "Why not me? Nathan's got it all over me—always has. He's brilliant. I'm smart, like a thousand other men, but Nathan—my God, Larry, Nathan's brilliant! He's the one you should have kept!"

"Look, Andy, try to understand. We had to give the two women tenure or there would have been the possibility of a class-action suit or some such thing. And you—why, Andy, we *had* to give it to you! My God, Andy. Your grandfather was the first history department head, and then there was your father. It's here waiting for you, Andy—this office. I'm still just keeping it warm for you."

Andrew stared at him, sickened. "You mean you'd give me tenure just because of who I am?"

"Why, of course, Andy, my boy! You're one of us. We always protect one of our own. You know that."

Andrew shook his head as if it were surrounded by fog. "But that means you give tenure to those who don't deserve it."

"What do you mean, don't deserve it? Of course you deserve it!"

"But what about Nathan? By any standard he's more deserving than I am."

Larry shrugged. "Those are the breaks, Andy. I'm just afraid those are the breaks."

"He's your sacrificial lamb, isn't he?" Andrew said, his anger now drained, replaced by a feeling of revulsion.

"Oh, now, Andy, boy, don't take it like that."

Andrew turned and walked out of the office, closing the door quietly behind him and heading back to his office. He found Nathan sitting at his desk, his feet up, his Asquith crimson-and-blue scarf wrapped jauntily around his neck as he guzzled rye from a bottle.

"Join me?" he asked gaily as he held the bottle up to Andrew.

Andrew stared. "Irma and Liz and I got it, Nathan. You were the one they let go."

Nathan smiled lightheartedly. "So join me in a drink, Andy, old buddy. A sort of farewell drink."

Andrew walked to the window, leaned his hands on the sill, and stared out at the campus. Spring had taken over. Everything was green, with patches of tulips and jonquils and late hydrangea, which would soon give way to lilacs, azaleas, and rhododendron. It was a beautiful campus, but its outward beauty hid an inner decay. It nauseated him. He sat down at his desk and scrawled a one-sentence letter, shoved it into an envelope, addressed it to Larry Hopewell, then got up, went over to Nathan, and took the bottle from his hand. He lifted it to his lips and let the rye burn down his throat, feeling as if it were washing away all the ugliness, all the decay, all that made him want to gag. Then he held the bottle out to Nathan and said, "Yes, Nathan, a farewell drink—for both of us."

Then he turned and, without further explanation, picked up the letter he'd just penned and walked down the hall to Larry Hopewell's office, where he placed the missive on his secretary's desk.

"See that he gets this, will you?" Andrew asked pleasantly. He then walked to his class, stood at the podium, and began his lecture, feeling at peace for the first time in months.

After his lecture, Andrew swung back to the office and found Nathan sitting at his desk, staring at his books, which were crammed into the bookshelves. Nathan acknowledged him with a glazed glance.

"I was just thinking about where I'll apply. I thought

I'd be here forever. I can't quite grasp it yet. All these books to be crated up and sent to another school..."

Andrew nodded sympathetically. "Look, why don't you bring Constance to dinner tonight. We can all talk then."

"What?" Nathan looked at Andrew as if seeing him for the first time. "Oh. Oh, sure. Dinner. What time?"

"Seven or thereabouts. It doesn't matter." He grinned. "Since I didn't give her any notice, Carrie will probably send out for pizza."

At that Nathan cheered up. "We'll be there. Make it pepperoni and mushrooms, okay?"

Andrew grinned. "It's a deal."

Carrie stared at Andrew. "You what?"

"I quit."

"You quit," she repeated dully, her mind filled with fuzzy wool. "You quit." She walked toward the fireplace in the study, then turned around and walked back to Andrew. "You quit?" Her eyes searched his, straining to see the truth. "But, Andrew, Asquith was your entire life. You always told me that."

"Yes, and I was a damned fool. I didn't realize it until a couple of weeks ago, when I stood in the quadrangle and listened to you speak. I saw then what I'd known subliminally for months now—that Asquith wasn't what I wanted. I'd been programmed for teaching history since I was a child, and I suddenly realized that it might have been what my parents wanted for me, but it wasn't what I wanted for myself."

He lifted Carrie's chin and smiled into her eyes. "I've been doing a lot of thinking lately, Carrie, looking into new fields, new careers. I'm thinking of training to be a stockbroker, in Hartford or New Haven perhaps. But in the meantime, while I'm still investigating things, I'd simply like to work with you in the bookstore. Would you mind if I wandered into your territory for a while, until I can get myself settled?"

Eyes glowing, Carrie looked up at her husband. "I'd love it. Andrew, I think it's wonderful—so long as it's what you really want. Since I saw you reading books about changing careers, I've been so afraid that it was *me* who was driving you out of Asquith. I'd put so much heat on you, what with my famous letters to the editor and protest marches."

He shook his head and gathered her into his arms. "Not a chance. You woke me up. It's a kind of reverse Sleeping Beauty story—the princess kissed the prince and he woke up and they lived happily ever after." He kissed her softly, their lips clinging together. He let his lips trail along her neck to her ear. She was wearing an old-fashioned dress of antique white lace, with a cameo at the high neckline, and he felt like sweeping her up into his arms and carting her off to the bedroom. But he looked at his watch and saw that seven was fast approaching.

"Darn," he said. "It's almost time for Constance and Nathan to arrive. I was kind of hoping we'd have time to start a baby." He looked out the windows at the spring flowers that surrounded the patio. The wrought-iron furniture had been brought out and was beckoning to them to sit and watch the sunset. Andrew grinned down at his wife. "I thought we might want to start a baby outside on the porch swing or under the bushes or some such place."

Carrie's eyes sparkled. "I'm afraid it's a little too late, Andrew."

He frowned, glancing at his watch. "I know. Not enough time. We'll have to hustle Constance and Nathan out of here as soon as we can."

"That's not what I meant," she said, eyes laughing. "We've already started one. In bed."

He stared at her, and slowly the meaning crept through the fog in his brain and made sense. "You mean...? You mean...?" He began to smile, holding her out from him and looking her up and down. "You don't look it."

"Well, good heavens, I only got it confirmed this morning!"

He pulled her into his arms, and they stood hugging each other, their laughter blending into a kiss. Then the doorbell rang.

"Damn. I wish I'd kept my big mouth shut about dinner tonight," Andrew groused.

Carrie give him a playful shove. "Go open the door and play the gracious host. I'll call and order a pizza to be delivered."

Andrew opened the door to Constance and Nathan and a surprise. A new Agatha Birdwell stood on the steps, glowing in a new suit and a becoming hairdo.

Andrew greeted Nathan and Constance, then drew Agatha in by the hand. "Why, Agatha, come in. What brings you here?" Then he held up a hand, yelling to Carrie, "Hey, make it an extra large pizza—Agatha Birdwell is here."

Agatha waved away his words. "Oh, I'm not going to stay. I just wanted to stop by and tell you my good news." She looked at Nathan and Constance, who stood smiling into each other's eyes, their arms around each other. "It looks like there's all sorts of good news tonight."

Carrie put down the phone and greeted everyone with a hug, then ushered them into the study. "Okay. Let's hear it."

Constance glowed. "Well, we told Daddy and Mama tonight. You should have seen Daddy's face when he realized he'd helped vote his future son-in-law out of getting tenure."

Carrie raised surprised brows. Andrew hadn't told her about Nathan not getting tenure. "Well, it doesn't seem to bother you two any."

Nathan grinned, pulling Constance closer. "We're already talking about where I'll apply. Yale, possibly, or Harvard."

Agatha Birdwell piped up. "You mean you two are getting married? Why, that's wonderful!" Then she shyly looked around. "I have some good news, too."

Everyone waited as Agatha cleared her throat and smoothed the skirt of her new suit over her knees. *"I'm* going back to school," she announced proudly. "I'm going to get my Master's and teach, if it's not too late."

There were choruses of congratulations, during which Agatha Birdwell beamed and returned the hugs that were bestowed on her. "I think it all began that night we had dinner here. I realized I'd spent my entire life doing what Oliver wanted me to. He told me what to wear, what to eat, and how to live. I couldn't help admiring Carrie, who seemed so alive and free. And I got to thinking, maybe it was time *I* started living my own life, too."

She sighed. "Of course, Oliver is a bit upset. He doesn't exactly know how to take my new independence." Then she smiled complacently. "He'll come around eventually, though."

Everyone broke into excited conversation, which was interrupted when the doorbell pealed and the pizza was delivered. They sat around the coffee table in the study, munching pizza and drinking wine. They were sipping coffee afterward when Andrew spoke up. "Well, I guess it's time we told you *our* news."

All heads turned toward him. He raised his coffee cup. "Here's to *my* new career. I've decided to leave Asquith. I'm thinking about becoming a stockbroker, but for the time being I'm going to work with Carrie in the bookstore." He smiled at her. "Which is going to work out just fine, since she just announced her intention of bringing another Everest into the world."

At that, pandemonium broke out, and everyone was laughing, hugging, and proposing toasts. Finally, about an hour later, everyone departed, leaving Carrie and Andrew alone at last.

Andrew closed the door after waving everyone good-bye, then took Carrie in his arms. "And now, Caroline Everest, there's someone I'd like you to meet."

Puzzled, Carrie let him lead her into the formal dining room. He flicked on the light that illuminated the portrait of his grandfather. Bewildered, Carrie looked from the portrait to Andrew.

"Carrie," he said quietly, "I'd like you to meet my grandfather. He earned the fortune that made it imperative that I learn to manage money and brought me inevitably to my real career—the stock market.

"And, Grandfather," he continued, "I'd like you to meet my wife, the new Mrs. Everest. She's not like your wife, or even my mother, but she's the most wonderful woman in the world, and I'm proud for you to meet her."

Tears welled up in Carrie's eyes. "Andrew," she whispered, going into his embrace. "How did you know that your family has always unnerved me? I've compared myself to them so often and come up wanting every time."

"You, my dear, are the best thing that's ever happened to the Everest clan."

She felt her soul fill with light and hugged Andrew hard. "Oh, I'm so very happy, darling." Then she looked up. "What'll we name the baby?"

"Oh, I don't know. Maybe we'll start a new tradition with names. Maybe we'll call him Oliver, after good old Ollie Birdwell."

Laughing, Carrie looked into her husband's eyes, secure in the knowledge that she was home at last. "Maybe we could think of something a bit more euphonious," she suggested dryly.

He flicked off the light over the portrait and led her to the door. "All right. Sidney then, or Grover, or Alfred—"

"And if it's a girl?" Carrie asked, laughing.

"Mehitabel."

In the dining room, someone seemed to chuckle . . .

WONDERFUL ROMANCE NEWS!

Do you know about the exciting SECOND CHANCE AT LOVE/TO HAVE AND TO HOLD newsletter? Are you on our *free* mailing list? If reading all about your favorite authors, getting sneak previews of their latest releases, and being filled in on all the latest happenings and events in the romance world sound good to you, then you'll love our SECOND CHANCE AT LOVE and TO HAVE AND TO HOLD Romance News.

If you'd like to be added to our mailing list, just fill out the coupon below and send it in…and we'll send you your *free* newsletter every three months — hot off the press.

☐ *Yes, I would like to receive your free*
SECOND CHANCE AT LOVE/TO HAVE
AND TO HOLD newsletter.

Name _____

Address _____

City _____ **State/Zip** _____

Please return this coupon to:

Berkley Publishing
200 Madison Avenue, New York, New York 10016
Att: Rebecca Kaufman

HERE'S WHAT READERS ARE SAYING ABOUT

To Have and to Hold™

"Your TO HAVE AND TO HOLD series is a fabulous and long overdue idea."
— *A. D., Upper Darby, PA**

"I have been reading romance novels for over ten years and feel the TO HAVE AND TO HOLD series is the best I have read. It's exciting, sensitive, refreshing, well written. Many thanks for a series of books I can relate to."
— *O. K., Bensalem, PA**

"I enjoy your books tremendously."
— *J. C., Houston, TX**

"I love the books and read them over and over."
— *E. K., Warren, MI**

"You have another winner with the new TO HAVE AND TO HOLD series."
— *R. P., Lincoln Park, MI**

"I love the new series TO HAVE AND TO HOLD."
— *M. L., Cleveland, OH**

"I've never written a fan letter before, but TO HAVE AND TO HOLD is fantastic."
— *E. S., Narberth, PA**

*Name and address available upon request

Second Chance at love ®

____07816-6	HEAD OVER HEELS #200	Nicola Andrews
____07817-4	BRIEF ENCHANTMENT #201	Susanna Collins
____07818-2	INTO THE WHIRLWIND #202	Laurel Blake
____07819-0	HEAVEN ON EARTH #203	Mary Haskell
____07820-4	BELOVED ADVERSARY #204	Thea Frederick
____07821-2	SEASWEPT #205	Maureen Norris
____07822-0	WANTON WAYS #206	Katherine Granger
____07823-9	A TEMPTING MAGIC #207	Judith Yates
____07956-1	HEART IN HIDING #208	Francine Rivers
____07957-X	DREAMS OF GOLD AND AMBER #209	Robin Lynn
____07958-8	TOUCH OF MOONLIGHT #210	Liz Grady
____07959-6	ONE MORE TOMORROW #211	Aimée Duvall
____07960-X	SILKEN LONGINGS #212	Sharon Francis
____07961-8	BLACK LACE AND PEARLS #213	Elissa Curry
____08070-5	SWEET SPLENDOR #214	Diana Mars
____08071-3	BREAKFAST WITH TIFFANY #215	Kate Nevins
____08072-1	PILLOW TALK #216	Lee Williams
____08073-X	WINNING WAYS #217	Christina Dair
____08074-8	RULES OF THE GAME #218	Nicola Andrews
____08075-6	ENCORE #219	Carole Buck
____08115-9	SILVER AND SPICE #220	Jeanne Grant
____08116-7	WILDCATTER'S KISS #221	Kelly Adams
____08117-5	MADE IN HEAVEN #222	Linda Raye
____08118-3	MYSTIQUE #223	Ann Cristy
____08119-1	BEWITCHED #224	Linda Barlow
____08120-5	SUDDENLY THE MAGIC #225	Karen Keast
____08200-7	SLIGHTLY SCANDALOUS #226	Jan Mathews
____08201-5	DATING GAMES #227	Elissa Curry
____08202-3	VINTAGE MOMENTS #228	Sharon Francis
____08203-1	IMPASSIONED PRETENDER #229	Betsy Osborne
____08204-X	FOR LOVE OR MONEY #230	Dana Daniels
____08205-8	KISS ME ONCE AGAIN #231	Claudia Bishop

All of the above titles are $1.95
Prices may be slightly higher in Canada.

Available at your local bookstore or return this form to:

SECOND CHANCE AT LOVE
Book Mailing Service
P.O. Box 690, Rockville Centre, NY 11571

Please send me the titles checked above. I enclose _____. Include 75¢ for postage
and handling if one book is ordered; 25¢ per book for two or more not to exceed
$1.75. California, Illinois, New York and Tennessee residents please add sales tax.

NAME_____

ADDRESS_____

CITY_____STATE/ZIP_____

(allow six weeks for delivery)   **SK-41b**